Goldie

"Move over, more. More." The director flicked his hand like he was shooing a fly away.

Goldie Hayes clenched her jaw and inched to the side, as directed. She would have furrowed her brow, but the amount of filler and Botox currently in her forehead made that impossible.

"*More.*" The wunderkind bro dude director was feeling very confident. Why wouldn't he? At twenty-eight, the studio had entrusted him with the next installment in the Victors Superhero Universe franchise. The VSU ruled the industry and had for nearly a decade.

The writing on the wall was in red capital letters. Trevor Sunday had no interest in making sure Goldie came out of this film with a single good scene; heck, probably not even a good frame.

She was standing there, in spandex, unable to bend or breathe, hands on her hips, her neck aching from the weight of the wig she was wearing, trying not to lose her temper.

Trevor Sunday wanted Piper Love in the center of the frame and Goldie Hayes out of it.

"P. Love, here." Trevor Sunday gently moved the glorious-looking Piper farther in front of Goldie.

"The side of Piper's head is going to be in my eye line for the close-up camera," Goldie pointed out. She had one line in this scene. But it was a good one, maybe even one that could make it into the trailers, the video game, and featured in the roller coaster ride being planned based on the movie inside the VSU park, set to open in Florida next year. Heck, one line, and she could be getting residuals for the rest of her life.

That was the upside to the indignity of all of this.

She had avoided superhero movies. She'd started out in indie movies, moved on to small roles in prestigious dramas, and had become successful in the rom-com genre. Not once had Goldie Hayes donned a superhero costume. But here she was. Her under boob area was starting to sweat in this costume. Did Wonder Woman have this issue?

Her agent promised her this line, this featured moment that could jump-start her current career stall. Trevor Sunday was unaware that this was important to her, or maybe he was. What he seemed most concerned about was the adoring gaze of Piper Love.

"The point of the scene is Piper. She's facing off with her father, Cromagnet. That's what's pivotal." Trevor was addressing Goldie's comment but gazing into Piper's eyes.

Ugh. Okay, well, this is how it was going to go.

Goldie needed that line, and she needed to look good while delivering it. She took a deep breath. And she embodied the sweetest disposition she could muster. She couldn't boss this twerp director. He had to feel like he was in charge.

"Trevor, what if you just shoot my line, full frame, for safety, and then do it again, with me here over to the side? That way, you have the sound and won't need me to come in and loop it later. But Piper will still be front and center. She should be."

Trevor tore his eyes from Piper and looked at Goldie for a moment.

Here was her chance.

"That's the way Tarantino did for it for Uma's big scene, gives you options, saves money, time. But I mean, of course, however you want me to do it. I can give you a couple of readings." She was making this up completely.

Goldie hated every single thing about having to kiss this kid's behind, but she needed that camera angle and to deliver her stupid summer blockbuster line.

"Okay, here's what we'll do. Tommy, keep her in the center for her line, then we do it with Piper center, so we see how she's affected rather than see the delivery. That's the choice that will make it edgier."

Goldie nodded; she'd get her shot. She looked at Tommy, the director of photography. He was an old friend. He saw every move she was making here. And he gave her a look that gave her hope. She saw him whisper into the ear of the camera operator. She took a breath.

Goldie would look good in this take. Tommy had her back. It could very well be cut. But at least she'd do everything possible to make it happen. Well, short of doing Trevor Sunday. She suspected, for him, she wasn't even rating in the MILF category.

Whatever.

Time for the line.

"Action!" It was go time.

Piper had the first line.

"I'm not your little girl anymore," Piper as Sparkle Dawn, budding superhero, defied the dictatorial Cromagnet, her father.

"You'll do as I command. I am CROMAGNET." Impressive reverberating audio would be added later. The actor playing Cromagnet wasn't even there. It was a stand-in.

But now, right here, this was Goldie's big moment, well, big second. She wasn't going to get sixty of them.

She lowered her chin, fixed a steely gaze at Cromagnet, and got into the stance she'd choreographed for days with the stunt coordinator. Steely Ann, her character, was a minor superhero from one issue of a comic book in the seventies. She was a throwaway, even in the comic books. But Goldie was going to do everything she could to make them remember her Steely Ann.

She used her lower register, the tone that brooks no debate, and she channeled a fierceness that wasn't acting.

The set, the costume, the ridiculous plot, all of it was artifice. But Goldie's heart was beating fast. Her mind was no longer riddled with worries about the external, her career, or how she looked. None of it mattered.

What mattered was that at this moment, she believed that Sparkle Dawn was her daughter and this jack wagon Cromagnet, her domineering ex-husband. In that framework, Goldie became Steely Ann, mother, protector, and fighter for the underdog.

She put her hand on the hilt of the prop sword of her costume. She looked at Cromagnet, stepped into her light, and delivered her line.

"You are Cromagnet. But I am the STEEL!" Goldie slid the sword from its scabbard. She sliced it in the air in front of her as if she was hacking through the vines of a malevolent forest.

Goldie sold the line. Tommy kept her in the center of the frame. She knew he'd likely push in on her eyes. They were flinty with determination.

This was why she had an Oscar. This was why they were lucky to have her in this dumpster fire movie. She didn't act. She felt it to her core. And everyone around her believed. She was totally committed to her role, to her line.

"Cut!"

Goldie nearly fell over with the weight of the swing she'd taken at Cromagnet's stunt double. She struggled to right herself.

"Thanks, Goldie, now move over. Let's go with about a foot."

Trevor didn't give her any feedback, compliment, or critique. He just needed her over to the side.

Goldie put the sword back in its scabbard. She stood where Trevor directed. They did the scene ten more times, but none of those takes included a close-up for Goldie.

She had her take, at least. Maybe someone higher up than Trever Sunday would like it, would see that she'd elevated the scene. Or not. Probably not. She'd done all she could do. But it probably was for nothing.

Tommy, the DP, caught up with her as she headed to her trailer. It took her about two hours to get the wig, the makeup, and the suit on. It took about thirty minutes to undo it all, with a team of three who were waiting inside.

"Hey, Goldie, you did well. That was a great read."

"Thanks for having my back."

"Of course."

That was nice. Nice was rare here. Tommy had run the camera on her first love scene back in the day. And he was never creepy about it. That was rare here, too.

She climbed into the trailer.

The wardrobe assistant worked on unzipping the back of her super suit. It was halfway down, and she was struggling out of the beast when Trevor appeared.

"Goldie, we've got a new take on the scene for tomorrow. I'm going to need you to look over these new lines. A bit different blocking."

Goldie was half in her robe and half in her super suit, and people were hovering all over her. She looked at the pages Trever gave her. She was also trying to ignore the rash that the spandex was causing under her armpits. She took the pages.

On the page, Steely Ann had gone from fighting next to Sparkle Dawn to being pushed down and helpless.

"Wait, I'm going land on my butt, and what's his name,

Greased Lighting or whatever, that sidekick character, is going to land *on top* of me?"

"It is going to be hilarious; he's going to give you a look, and then you'll sort of give it back to him. Like you're interested. You know, kind of a superhero cougar thing. Funny, right?"

"I don't like it; you're turning her into comic relief. From all my research, she's a role model, or is supposed to be."

"Please, she was a one-off. Think about it. This will be sexy and funny. Maybe get some of the fans into older women. You're welcome."

Trevor was doing this to get her back. Pure and simple. She'd stood up for herself, for her one good take, and he was punishing her by turning her into a joke, turning her scenes into parodies.

"It's not funny or sexy. It's just demeaning."

Trevor took a step forward; he lowered his voice. A sneer curled his upper lip.

"You are used goods. No one gives a crap about your movies. You're in this because some doddering studio exec had a crush on you in the nineties. Probably before I was born."

Goldie wanted to slap his face, she wanted to spit, she wanted to tell him to take his superhero movie and shove it up his Fortress of Solitude.

He took a step forward, looming over her, with all pretenses of respect gone.

"Did you hear me? I do not want you here. So, if I tell you to kiss a mutant rottweiler in the next scene, you'll do it, or you're out on your ancient arse."

Goldie put her hands up. It was a reflex, as though she was being assaulted. But he kept at it.

"I have a vision, and it doesn't have grandparent superheroes."

That was such a joke. She was old, but half the actors who played superheroes in this cast were older than she was.

Goldie flung herself around. She did not want to be near this man.

"Get out of my trailer. I don't have to take this!"

As she flung around, dramatically, of course, the back of her hand made contact with Trevor's lacky assistant. Who knows what Derek's job was, but he was always carrying things for Trevor.

"Ow, oh, oh she hit me!"

"What?"

"You scratched me. You psycho diva, you scratched my face!"

"I'm sorry, I—"

Goldie looked at Trevor. He seemed happy, victorious even, at this little mishap.

Uh great. He was going to make that the thing.

"It's okay. Menopause did the same thing to my mom."

Goldie was done with this little jerk, done with this job, done with this town.

"Get out. I'm not doing the scene. I'm not doing any more scenes in this piece of crap movie!"

"Fine by me. I'm sure the studio will be happy to take back the millions you're getting for a few minutes of airtime. Or maybe Derek's lawyer will."

Great, a threat now.

Trevor skittered out of the trailer, supporting Derek as though he'd been nearly killed by the errant brush of her hand.

She was 5' 2" and tipped the scales at a whopping 110 pounds, but sure, she really hurt that full-grown man.

Goldie intended to run to the door and scream an epithet at the director, but she forgot she was still half locked into the tight, constricting, totally ridiculous superhero costume.

She tripped on her way to the door and hit the makeup table on her way down. Brushes and tubes when flying, and she landed with a thud.

There was no complete silence in the small space as the makeup assistant, wardrobe assistant, and wig master stared down at her.

"Get this stupid thing off me!" She lifted her legs, and three assistants did their best to extricate her from the suit.

The entire episode was humiliating and infuriating and left Goldie unsure of what to do next. She'd always been sure when it came to her work.

By the next day, the story of Goldie Hayes' behavior was all over TMZ, TikTok, and Twitter. She was the temperamental aging has-been actress who didn't understand the vision of the hot shot cool bro dude director.

She'd slapped an underling and trashed her trailer. That was what everyone was saying.

That was what everyone thought. That's what Trevor's army of rabid fanboys believed.

She supposed either Trevor or maybe Derek had leaked the totally inaccurate story to the tabloids.

But people were buying it.

She *was* an aging has-been actress.

And the career she'd given everything to was being drowned out by noise she couldn't stop.

Chapter Two

Libby

"Wow, this place is amazing. Is this how the other half lived?" J.J. said as her friends toured the old Two Lakes Grove Hotel.

"Well, if by other half you mean a family of raccoons, I think they've taken up residence in the attic."

Libby wanted J.J. and Hope's take on the place and on her plan to lure their old friend Goldie to Irish Hills.

The Two Lakes Grove Hotel was built around the same time as Nora House. It was, as advertised, atop a hill, in a grove of trees, and situated on the narrow stretch of land adjacent to the channel that connected the two lakes, Manitou and Round.

"Look, Goldie has a fabulous life and mansion of her own in L.A. I think we need to do something more to make coming here seem like a good idea."

Aunt Emma had given Libby the push to approach Goldie. The same push had worked out spectacularly with Hope. But Libby was less confident she could convince Goldie that Irish Hills was a good investment.

"What did you have in mind?" Hope asked.

"Okay, so this place would be an investment. I'll pitch that for sure. But what about a Goldie Hayes Film Festival?"

"Oh, I love that," Hope said.

"What's involved in a film festival? I've never been to one," J.J. said.

"Well, it can be a place for new artists to share their work or big studios like at Cannes in France, but I was thinking, just an appreciation weekend. I think we can pull that off fast. She's a big star with a tie to our little town. We'd be the perfect place to host something like that."

"Lure her here. Maybe she brings some of her Hollywood friends," said J.J.

"Right, and we do it over North of Nash Festival weekend. Since there's already a huge contingent of fans and country music stars in the area."

North of Nash was held at Michigan International Speedway in nearby Brooklyn, Michigan. The event was huge. It was as if aliens teleported Nashville to Michigan for three days with beer. There had to be a way to get some of that tourism money and traffic to downtown Irish Hills.

"Is there a crossover, country stars, fans, and Goldie Hayes?" J.J. asked.

"She did win the Oscar for the Brenda Lee biopic, so maybe," Libby pointed out. She knew from her days as the organizer of big fundraisers that once you got one big name, others were easier to add. Liz Gould, their Sandbar Sister, now Goldie Hayes, Superstar, was as big a name as you could get. Despite her recent bad publicity.

"True, so what can we do?" Hope asked.

"Wish me luck, and oh, I need someone to take on repairs. Even if she says no, it won't be wasted. I need to sell this thing, and before that, I need it showable."

In a lot of ways, Two Lakes Grove was perfect. The potential was enormous. It also took up a prime location. If Stirling Stone could buy it, he would. But instead, it sat in the sagging real estate portfolio that Libby and Aunt Emma were trying to support. If they officially put it on the market, Stone would grab it and tear it down. Libby knew it. For now, to get it off her books, she'd need to get it sold on the sly.

But before that, it needed some sprucing.

"Anyway, Dean said he knew a guy who could start work on the repairs here?"

"Yep, Dean and I can get that end sorted out. The contractor he's thinking of might need to stay on the premises. He's just back in the area." J. J. was always willing to jump in on anything Libby needed.

"Great, yes. Do whatever it takes to get stuff started. There's a caretaker cottage, plus the dozen rooms in the hotel itself. We need to get this place sold. I don't think I can wait too long with it on my balance sheet. Even if Goldie isn't interested, I must get the hotel off my hands."

Libby and her aunt owned too many dilapidated properties; this one was one of the largest. And it was more neglected than dilapidated. This hotel was a gem, but it could easily be destroyed by raccoons or rain if they didn't get going on it. Libby needed cash; more than that, she needed it from the right places.

Libby saw every repair, every rehab she managed, as a victory against Stirling Stone. She'd seen the plans. This place would be a casino if he had his way.

The hotel here was beautiful, stately, but you couldn't back one thousand tourists in here, not by a mile. There were twelve rooms, huge for the time, but nothing compared to what Stone was planning.

"What's my assignment?" Hope asked.

"You're up to your neck at the restaurant," Libby said.

Hope had only been open for two weeks. It had gone great. Hope served people the best meals of their lives at Hope's Plate.

But there weren't enough people, that was the thing. Libby was determined to draw tourists to Irish Hills.

"You know, I did cater. What about this? If you get in front of Goldie, let her know that she doesn't have to worry about a continental breakfast. Braylon and I will work up something that can be delivered here five days a week. He's amazing with pastry."

"Great. Work it up, budgets, and everything. Though I have to get her here first. Spring the buying the hotel idea second? Ugh, it's all a long shot."

"Yep."

"So, when is your flight?" J.J. asked.

"Tomorrow morning, wish me luck?"

"Just channel Aunt Emma's energy, and Goldie won't be able to refuse."

Aunt Emma had positioned Libby here, and with her guidance, Libby had maneuvered Hope into staying and joining the fight to save Irish Hills.

Goldie was a different story. She was a movie star, had a gorgeous mansion, and probably everything she dreamed about when she used to hang with them on Lake Manitou.

Libby had to bet on the fact that no matter how fabulous Goldie's life was, there was something unique about this place and the bond shared by the Sandbar Sisters.

If that didn't work, maybe Aunt Emma had dirt on her. That's how she convinced Libby. Ha, no, no.

Libby would just make her a few offers, good offers. That would work.

It had to!

Chapter Three

Goldie

"They're going to sue you."

Scott Ozock, Goldie's agent, sat on her twenty-thousand-dollar sofa. It faced an expanse of windows that showed off an infinity pool that blended seamlessly into her spectacular view of L.A.

But the man was essentially pooing all over the fancy sofa with every sentence.

Goldie couldn't sit. All she could do was pace. It felt like she was watching her hard work over the last three decades slip between her fingers.

"What?"

"Yeah, the assistant has facial scarring."

"You have got to be kidding me! I accidentally made contact, and there wasn't even a scratch on him. Meanwhile, Trevor was being abusive, insensitive, unprofessional, and I will not take it."

"No one in this town believes it."

"They believe the gossip, the stuff on Twitter. Great. Of course. The five-foot-two, one hundred pound geriatric actress beat the heck out of the twenty-something, six-foot-tall man child. Makes sense."

"He mentioned something about pills?"

"What?"

"Yeah, there was a bottle of pills you made an assistant get, that with the coming unhinged thing, well. It's bad."

"I forgot to take my estrogen, which I'm on thanks to my hysterectomy. Estrogen!"

"Ah, female stuff."

No one outside of her closest circle knew about Goldie's hysterectomy. While the P.R. machine in this town loved to talk about the disease of the week, menopause and "female stuff" did not make for great copy. In fact, she'd stayed quiet, especially so the bro dude directors didn't mistake her for their mothers. Any chance at lead roles were history if she became the poster girl for getting a hysterectomy.

Her agent wanted her to keep quiet about it. And she had. She did what was required to stay at the top of the heap in Hollywood.

She needed Scott Ozock's father, not Scott. He'd have squished this director like a bug.

Goldie clenched her jaw and continued to pace. She needed a plan. She needed to look like she had something better to do than this stupid superhero movie.

Mitchell Ozock had been Goldie's agent since her second year in Hollywood. He ruled this town in the early nineties. He got her the role in *Beautiful Girl* that turned her into a household name. The blockbuster receipts of that film turned Mitchell Ozock, talent agent, into Mitchell Ozock, studio head.

Mitchell Ozock, in her corner, was a key to her rise. He had seen her small role in *The Sandwich Shop*, a low-budget but well-reviewed indie picture.

He'd championed her to play Oberlin Banks' daughter in *Dark Homecoming*. Banks won her second Oscar for that picture.

Mitchell then pushed to get Goldie the lead in *Beautiful Girl*.

All of it unfolded in less than four years after she showed up in L.A. with one shampoo commercial and a bit part in a television movie on her resume.

Her face was on billboards all over town, thanks to *Beautiful Girl.*

That was how much she owed Mitchell Ozock. She owed him enough to let Ozock the lesser continue on as her agent. Scott Ozock had a lot of power now, too, which he owed to his deal with the Victor Superhero Universe. But what he didn't have was loyalty to Goldie. They didn't have the bond like Goldie had with his dad.

All those movies that made her career felt like they were filmed a million years ago. They could be silent pictures for all the Trevor Sundays of the world knew.

She'd made a powerful ally in Mitchell Ozock, but he was gone now. He'd died of a heart attack eight years ago. And it was downhill ever since for Goldie.

His son, Scott Ozock, was her age. They'd known each other forever. But that didn't mean he was doing anything in her best interest. That, and Goldie's age, meant she was in the worst position of her career.

"That's not all. I have other, uh, news."

"I've been essentially booted from the most powerful movie franchise on the planet. Worse? What could be worse?"

Scott hesitated. He looked down at her marble flooring. He stalled further by gazing at the infinity pool over Goldie's shoulder.

He then looked down at his shoes.

"I have to drop you."

"You must be joking. You're *dropping me*? You're the one who put me in that picture, told me to get that line. Fight."

This was impossible to process. Goldie had carried this guy! She'd stayed with him out of loyalty to his father, and he was dropping her?

"The thing is, we're a part of the whole talent package for the movie and for the next three. The director wants you gone, or if not, we lose the sequel and the prequel."

"Now I wish I *had* scratched someone's eyes out."

Scott got up and started to make his way out of Goldie's house.

To call it a house was an understatement. Goldie had a mansion, a mid-century masterpiece. It was in the tony neighborhood of the Trousdale Estates.

It was gorgeous. It was the perfect setting for the status she'd acquired. She lived here with Myrna, her Bichon. But despite its size, there was no husband, no kids filling the massive square footage.

This was the sacrifice she'd made to be at the top. This was the path she'd voluntarily chosen. The marble floors felt like quicksand under her feet.

"The papers are being sent to your attorney. We'll be dissolving all ties. You understand, don't you? It's the VSU. We can't lose those deals."

"Scott, your dad would never have let this happen to me."

"He's gone, and I'm sorry. So are you, for all intents and purposes."

Scott stood up from her fancy sofa. He turned his back on Goldie and walked out. Goldie was livid. How in the heck had it come to this? In one moment?

"I'm not being dropped, Scott—oh no, I'm dropping you!!"

Myrna ran through the hallway and out the door as Goldie's emotions spiraled out of control.

She was panicked, angry, and in disbelief. And she felt betrayed. Her years of loyalty to Mitchell Ozock and his measly son had evaporated thanks to a disagreement with the latest bratty director.

Scott didn't look back as she hurled her toothless statement at him.

Goldie was dropped.

Well, she'd find another agent, or an indie project, or a script to invest in. Why in the world hadn't she started buying rights to books like Winne Reese did? She hadn't gotten into producing. Ugh. She was at the mercy of an industry that valued her for her figure, face, and ability to turn on a fifteen-year-old boy. It was a mess!

She walked out to the pool and looked out. The view alone here was worth a million dollars. It was the right view in the right neighborhood.

This was where Hollywood power players lived. She walked among them! She had an Oscar, for flip's sake.

Was this it? Should she start again? Tears stung the corners of her eyes, but she blinked them away. No. She was way tougher than that.

No one got here without being tough. She just hadn't been quite smart enough. She should have seen this.

She'd ignored the signs that Scott Ozock wasn't operating in her best interests. They had boxed her out of an agency that used to use her name to recruit top talent.

Goldie didn't know how long she stood there, looking at L.A. spread out below her. This view used to fill her with satisfaction. It was the proof she'd made it.

But right now, it made her feel cold. It made her feel alone. Millions of people out there and not one she could call to vent. Or to come over and commiserate.

She'd isolated herself on purpose.

Goldie was upset, betrayed, disappointed, and frustrated.

But she was also a fighter. She'd come here alone and had done what it took to get ahead. Despite how she was marketed in half her pictures, she wasn't a delicate little thing.

She looked like a waif most of the time, but she wasn't. Even though bile was the only thing she'd swallowed for three weeks leading up to fitting into that stupid super suit.

She had literally starved herself to be Steely Ann. All for her one stupid line. She couldn't remember the last time she had a full stomach. It was all so messed up.

Her mind was drawing a blank, though, on how to proceed, on what to do next.

A voice pulled her out of her head and back poolside.

"Goldie, is this your little gal? I'm sorry, but the door was open, and she trotted right up to me."

Goldie turned to find a gorgeous woman with waves of long auburn hair walking out to the patio. Myrna tucked in her arm. This had to be a former supermodel or something. Did Goldie forget some sort of charity event committee meeting?

"Myrna!" Goldie rushed forward, and the woman gently handed her over.

"Goldie, I'm so sorry to just show up. I know it's weird."

"Excuse me?"

Maybe this a stalker? Did she need to find her panic button? Hollis, her driver, was also security. Where was he? Oh great, in the middle of her greatest professional disaster, she was going to get murdered. Though, maybe that would be good, in terms of P.R. She'd get posthumous adoration!

No, no. She wasn't ready for posthumous adoration quite yet. Goldie stepped back but dialed into the woman who'd walked into her home unannounced. She did not look unbalanced, and she had just gently handed her back Myrna Loy.

Quality clothing, real gold earrings, a tasteful tennis bracelet. She looked more country mansion than Charles Manson. The woman was tall. She had a lovely long neck, thick auburn hair, and eyes that flashed with intelligence. Familiar eyes.

And then a rush of decades zoomed through her mind. She knew who this was.

"*Libby Quinn?*"

"Yes, hey Goldie. It's been a long time."

Goldie was not a hugger. She had cultivated a way to keep personal space. First, it was to keep pawing casting directors at arm's length. Later, the fans, who thought they knew, thought they were owed a piece of her, needed to be kept back. Sometimes they grabbed at her to collect what they thought was due to them for being her fans.

Libby did not know this version of Goldie. Libby's version of Goldie hugged, kissed, swam, and did all things, full-throated and raw. Surviving in Hollywood required a glossy veneer.

Most people wanted something from Goldie. She'd learned how to deflect that. Hugging strangers or old friends was not in her playbook these days.

Libby smiled at her.

"You grew up gorgeous," Goldie said.

"Ha, you were always. I've missed you."

"Yes, well, it's been a long time."

Goldie's well-learned skeptical attitude returned. What was this woman doing here? They may have been BFFs before the term BFFs was invented, but they were strangers now.

"It has. We're all so proud of you. J.J. said she—how did she put it?—spit out her popcorn when she saw you in *The Sandwich Shop*."

"J.J., how is she? I mean, she was so vibrant!"

Goldie thought back to her friend, J.J. She tapped into the memory of J.J. when she needed to play fearless characters. There was quite a bit of J.J. in Goldie's interpretation of Brenda Lee.

"She's still a firecracker, hasn't changed."

"Ah, well, that's good to know." Goldie realized she was probably being a bad hostess.

"I know I am here unannounced."

"No, it's fine, have a seat. I'll get Tally to get us some cold drinks."

Tally was her current personal assistant and Gal Friday. She went through them quickly, but Tally had lasted over a year.

"Oh, don't go to any trouble—"

"Please, it's not. TALLY!" Goldie yelled, and Tally appeared on the patio.

"Yep, what can I get you?" Tally was in her twenties, originally from Chicago, good at explaining TikTok to her and mediocre at returning phone calls.

"Can you bring us two cucumber waters and take Myrna?"

"Hey, you're Libby Malcolm," Tally said, clearly recognizing Libby.

What had Goldie missed? Was Libby famous or something?

"Yes," Libby said and lowered her head a bit.

"I grew up in Southland! My mom's still there. I did the Sunday Art in the Park for years. And that was total crap, what your ex did."

"I'm so glad you enjoyed the program. That makes me really happy. And thank you."

"Wow, Libby Malcolm, I never know who I'm going to meet in this job. Last week I ran into Suzanne Somers when I was picking up Goldie's green matcha powder."

"Tally, could you?" Goldie put the dog in Tally's arms and ended the girl's rambling grocery shopping with the stars tour.

"Oh, yes, sorry. Again, honored to meet you, Libby."

"Well, so you're famous," Goldie said. "I had no idea."

Goldie knew that sounded mean, dismissive. It was another trick one picked up in her status-obsessed business. *Oh, you're an actress. Would I have seen you in anything?*

"Not really, maybe in Southland Neighborhood board meetings in Chicagoland. Though I did meet Bono once."

"He's so little, right? I mean, a giant in the world, but so little?"

"I did feel rather monstrous sized next to him."

They laughed. There was an ease, a familiarity, that Goldie was surprised to feel. Surprised to be warmed by.

"So, Chicago, community organizer, hanging out with Bono

—what's next, a bid for president? Are you here for my celebrity endorsement?"

"Ha, no, you missed that second part. My husband, ex-husband, nearly got me sent to prison when he embezzled from my non-profit. So, yeah, not interested in high office. But I am going to admit that I am still a community organizer. Just a different community."

Here it was, here was the ask. Goldie liked to support charity. She'd walked the red carpet at tons of fundraisers.

"How much do you need? I'm happy to donate. Though you may not want my endorsement for whatever. My name isn't great right now."

"What I want is to honor you at the First Annual Goldie Hayes Film Festival, to be held in Irish Hills."

"Shut up, that's hilarious. And Irish Hills, that place was wiped off the map, right? After the tornado."

Her parents had moved to Florida after the tornado. There had never been a reason to go back. And honestly, once she started making it big, everyone just wanted to visit her here. Why wouldn't they?

"Well, almost. So let me put all my cards on the table. I've moved back to Irish Hills, well, maybe ran away to Irish Hills after my husband dragged my name through the mud. And the place turned into my mission. I'm working to save it, and well, it's a cliché for sure, but it's saving me, too."

"Oh, brother, that's Hallmark Movie dialogue right there," Goldie said. It was probably too harsh. She was used to harshness. She was used to rudeness. That was show business.

"I know, but it doesn't mean it isn't true."

"I'm sorry, I didn't mean to be, well, me."

"It's cool, really, and what I have in mind is nutty. I made a similar offer to Hope just a few weeks ago."

Hope Benton. Strong, self-assured, and tall. Those were the

things that flashed in her mind about those long ago summers with Hope, J.J., Viv, and Libby.

"Hope, wow. I'm sure she's a fantastic chef by now?"

"Yes, yes, she is. But it was a recent development. She just opened the most amazing place in downtown Irish Hills."

"Cute!"

"So, this is the deal. Irish Hills needs you. Straight up. The town is fighting extinction, and it needs you. Irish Hills needs a dose of your glamour, your celebrity, and the sparkle you bring. And I'm not going to lie. It's crass, but Irish Hills needs to hitch its wagon to your star."

Goldie was used to people asking her to lend her name to things. It was part of her worth in the world, she figured.

"My fading star, tarnished star."

"Please, you're a household name. And look, yeah, we need your star power in Irish Hills. But more importantly, we need you back with our little Sandbar Sisters girl squad. And I think you need us, too."

"Hmm, does it look like I'm suffering here, missing something?" Goldie put out her hands expansively to the million-dollar view in her million-dollar mansion. She felt hollow when she did it. Libby was someone who wasn't impressed with this kind of artifice. Goldie knew it. She always knew it.

"No, it's beautiful. In my case, and in Hope's, Irish Hills was a refuge, financial, emotional, and spiritual, in a lot of ways. I can see you don't need that. But maybe it would be good to get back with a group of people who knew you way back when. People that don't care about your recent dust-up with the Victor Superhero Universe."

"Yeah, you heard about that," Goldie said.

Everyone had heard about it. What no one knew yet, was that after thirty years in Hollywood, Goldie, movie star, and Oscar winner, was agentless.

"Well, TMZ does get to Michigan."

"Ah, yes, well, look. I appreciate the offer. But I've got a career crisis going on. And I need to deal with it. I have to be here to strategize and find a new agent. Talk to an attorney on some things. I just can't do a film festival all the way in Michigan. In fact, I actually have to get going. I'm set to appear at Dream Factory Comic Con in like less than two hours."

"Oh, I'm so sorry. I did barge in on you."

"No, no, I'm glad to see you. I want to catch up. But I am already getting a reputation for being a diva. This autograph and photo session at the Comic Con is important. If I don't show, well, it will prove them all right."

"I'll get out of your way. I totally understand."

Goldie did want to catch up, and despite the development of her thick skin, and tough Hollywood outer shell, part of her wanted to open up. In her heart, she was starting to see what her life was missing. It was friends like she had growing up on Lake Manitou.

She'd never let anyone in like she did then. But it was likely way too late now. Even so, she had an idea.

"I don't know if you have other plans or anything, but would you like to go with me to this comic con event? It's kind of fun to see the frenzy at these things."

"I'd love it."

"I must warn you; it can also give you a major headache. Loud, big, crowded, and filled with just, well, stuff. It's not relaxing, but it is a show."

"I'm in."

"Great, TALLY! Tell the team I'm on the way."

"Team?"

"Hair and makeup are standing by at the Anaheim Convention Center, they'll spruce me up, and we're all set."

"Got it."

Goldie was disproportionately happy about Libby agreeing to

hang out for a bit at the Comic Con. She should be worried about Scott, the VSU, and her career.

But instead, she was going to get to find out what happened to her old Sandbar Sisters.

It would be a great way to distract her from the crap Scott and Trevor were slinging in her direction.

Chapter Four

Libby

Libby marveled at how ageless Goldie was. They were all around fifty, the Sandbar Sisters, but Goldie, she was timeless. And tiny, Goldie was always petite, but she looked more birdlike now, like her skin barely held her bones together. And even that was tenuous.

She portrayed a tough exterior, but Libby knew the girl. She knew the bright penny that was Liz Gould, now Goldie Hayes.

Despite that, Goldie talked tough and fast. Libby couldn't even imagine how savvy her old friend had to be to rise to the top like she had.

Goldie's driver, Hollis, got them to the Anaheim Convention Center.

It looked like a spaceship, landed in the middle of a row of hotels, Libby thought.

Hollis left to park the vehicle. Tally, carrying whatever gear Goldie required, led the way as they went up a back elevator to an attached suite above the massive convention center.

Libby watched as people scurried around, focused on making sure Goldie had what she needed. There was an entire category of employment in L.A. that made a living scurrying around movie stars. And it appeared Goldie had some of the best of them. By the time hair and makeup finished with Goldie, she looked radiant. The movie star was there, in front of Libby, where the old friend had been.

"Wow, you do not age."

"Ha, yeah, right, this is a careful combination of science, engineering, and alchemy," Goldie said as she circled her face with her hand.

The event staff knocked on the door.

"The booth is ready for you, Ms. Hayes."

"Hmm, can you wait a moment? My security team isn't here yet."

"Well, we have event security, and the time slots are super tight."

"Okay, okay. Tally, can you be sure to text Hollis?"

"Yes, of course."

Libby, Tally, and the event coordinator comprised Goldie's entourage as they made their way to Hall B.

Goldie kept her head down, almost as if she was hiding. As if she read Libby's mind, Goldie whispered an explanation.

"If too many people see you walk to the space, it can cause a ruckus, and then the fans who paid for the autograph sessions and picture sessions get enraged," Goldie said. And she gave Libby a wink.

"Makes sense."

They walked through the huge spaces that comprised the massive Anaheim Convention Center.

"This place looks like something out of *Star Trek*," Libby commented.

The event coordinator answered, "Actually, it is. They used this for exteriors and some interiors for Star Fleet."

"Ah, well, I can see why."

They snaked through the crowd. Libby had long legs, Goldie did not, but it was Goldie who set the fast pace.

They wound up at a row of tables at the end of the room. Clear plexiglass separated stations, where a celebrity sat at an elevated table. The line of fans, snaking through a rope maze, offered up an item up to the celebrity to sign.

Libby tried not to gawk at famous faces in the neighboring autograph areas. There was an action star she recognized, a beloved character actor, and even a celebrated comic book writer, all lined up, greeting fans.

They were each booked for one hour. Only fans who'd reserved time and purchased a special ticket were guaranteed a picture and autograph.

Libby stepped back out of the way as Tally opened a water bottle for Goldie, and the event coordinator used a walkie-talkie to communicate, presumably with some central organization office for the event.

"You ready, Ms. Hayes?"

"Fire away," said Goldie. She turned to Libby. "If this gets boring, wander around. It's the best people watching in the world at these things. You might even get some free swag!"

For the first time since they'd left her house, the megawatt smile of Goldie Hayes appeared, and it lit up her face. In Libby's estimation, it could light up the entire hall. That smile turned Goldie Hayes right back into the spitting image of a teenage Liz Gould.

"Attention, Dream Factory Comic Con! Superstar Goldie Hayes is in the building! If you're signed up for a session, head to Hall B for a picture and autograph!"

Libby felt a shift in the air. It was electric.

Disorganized milling about from the crowd beyond the ropes turned into something solid, a mass of people pushing forward to see Goldie.

She worried for a moment that Goldie's bodyguard hadn't made it back yet. Even fans who loved Goldie could be a little scary. This whole thing was a bit chaotic. It was wonderful, but it was also one click on the dial away from hysteria, Libby thought.

It was fascinating, but also it made Libby long for the quiet of the lake. This was going to be bananas.

The line formed, and the first few people approached Goldie. She smiled and signed posters, books, dolls, and whatever they presented to her from her movies.

But then, the crowd here increased in size but decreased in age. Libby noticed a preponderance of Victor Superhero Universe t-shirts and merch, as they called it.

Libby watched as a worried Tally leaned over Goldie.

"Uh, you're blowing up on Twitter," Tally said and handed her phone to Goldie.

Goldie read the tweets aloud.

"Goldie Hayes dropped. Studio set to sue. Next, VSU movie delayed thanks to Goldie Haye's antics."

"This is gonna be a thing, I think," Tally said. There was a grimace on the assistant's face as she looked out toward the crowd amassing to approach Goldie.

"Yeah, and the rabid fanboys are jumping all over me on here. They want their next installment, and they want it now."

Goldie handed the phone back to Tally.

Libby watched as a man, who looked to be in his twenties, with a Cromagnet Forever t-shirt on, walked up to Goldie.

"You WITCH!!! YOU RUINED THE FRANCHISE, AND WE'RE NOT GETTING OUR SPARKLE MOVIE PREVIEW!"

He threw his water bottle at Goldie and water sprayed Goldie and Tally.

Libby leaped forward.

"Hey, you little jerk. Back off!"

The swarm of people pressing forward didn't look enraptured to meet a celebrity. They looked angry.

"Team TREVOR!"

"What? Team Trevor?" Goldie asked Tally.

"Justice for Trevor!" This was another shout from the crowd.

"Hashtag, yeah, worldwide trend, along with—"

"What?"

"GetGoldieGone."

"Oh, boy," Libby said.

As soon as Tally was done uttering the words, the same phrase rose above the general din of voices in the convention hall.

"Get Goldie Gone, Get Goldie Gone."

The crush of fans knocked over the rope maze designed to control the crowd.

Something else flew through the air. This time, it was some sort of blonde doll. Had it hit someone, it would have hurt. It bounced off the plexiglass.

"Let's go," Libby said. She put her hand out to Goldie, and Goldie took it. But she looked unsure.

"I contracted to do this. I can't leave."

"That group wants to tear you apart," Libby said.

Goldie stood up. A loud round of boos filled the space.

"Hey, this movie delay isn't on me," Goldie said. It was useless to try to argue with this mob.

"You're a hag!!!!!"

Goldie looked confused, hurt, and like a deer in the headlights.

"Tally, grab her stuff," Libby said as she took charge. She put an arm around Goldie and tried to shield her from the debris now coming their way in irregular intervals.

It looked like old movie posters of Goldie's, a stuffed animal from the animated feature she'd voiced, and food.

"Good Lord, someone's setting my poster on fire."

The smell of smoke started to permeate the room. An alarm went off.

"We need to go." Libby wasn't taking no for an answer now.

Goldie was stunned, in shock, and it appeared that she was paralyzed by the unfolding fanboy chaos coming her way. This woman was used to being adored, Libby realized.

She needed to get Goldie moving.

"Where in the heck is Hollis?" Tally said. As though the crowd would hold off until the beefy security guard arrived.

Libby looked at Goldie. Her Botox had apparently broken loose because her face was no longer a smooth mask of dewy glamour but more like a contorted caricature of shock.

"Elizabeth Gould, snap out of it. We need to haul ass like the groundskeeper's chasing us off the ninth green."

That did it. Goldie shook her head and blinked. "Yeah, let's go."

Libby weaved around the other celebrities, who had the protection of security teams.

She guided them back behind the backdrop of the autograph stations. The swell of the crowd would knock those things down if it got any uglier.

"There, there's the exit!" Tally yelled.

Libby saw it.

"Get Goldie Gone, Get Goldie Gone!" The chant got closer.

Libby looked back toward the roped-off area. It was now overrun with angry fans of the VSU.

"This way!" They heard a deep voice call to them and motion them over.

It was Hollis, Goldie's driver. He had a service door propped open. The door led to the backstage area of the hall. Convention-goers didn't have access to the bowels of the building, thank goodness, thought Libby.

Hollis held the door with one hand and had his phone out with the other.

Libby wondered for a split second why he'd be doing that,

taking pictures. But it passed out of her brain in favor of the survival instinct to get Goldie out of there.

They nearly sprinted for five more minutes until they found themselves at the loading dock. Goldie's car was waiting.

Hollis opened the car door, and the three women piled in. They were silent, working to manage their heart rates, and Tally kept looking out the rear window of the SUV.

As they drove away from the convention, Libby glanced at Goldie as her old friend processed the last few minutes.

"They are usually clamoring at that thing, but it's to be nice to me, to tell me their favorite movie."

"Well, looking at Twitter, it appears Trevor has weaponized his fan base. It's all your fault they're not getting what they want," Tally said.

"Are you okay?" Libby put her hand out and squeezed Goldie's.

"I, yeah, I am. I need to get home, get a drink maybe, call my agent. Wait, he just dropped me."

On the drive back to Goldie's exclusive Trousdale neighborhood, they looked at Twitter and read headlines deriding Goldie Hayes.

"Ms. Hayes, what do you want me to do here?" Hollis said.

The women peaked out of the tinted window at the drive to Goldie's estate. About two dozen Victor Superhero Universe fans were there, with signs and chanting the same stupid thing.

"We can't go in there," Libby said.

"I need to get out of town," Goldie said.

She was finding her voice again. That was good. Her friend had been stunned by the turn of events. But she was rallying.

"Where to?" Hollis asked.

"Chateau Marmont, I can hold up in a bungalow," Goldie said. "Tally, we're going to drop you off next door. Ellen's staff knows you. You can sneak around to my place. I need you to pack for me."

"What do you need?"

"The standard two-week stuff, like I had for Cannes last year."

"Got it."

Hollis drove one spot over, and Tally exited.

By the time they got to the Chateau Marmont in West Hollywood, Goldie was more tiger than deer in headlights. She was mad. Libby saw this as a good sign.

"I cannot believe that little snake, cannot believe it. My career is up in flames over one bro dude director. It's outrageous. I wonder if I should call *Variety*. Offer my side?"

She was throwing a million ideas out. It was a spaghetti fling of P.R. campaigns, and Libby mostly just listened. Goldie needed to burn off the adrenaline of the last few hours being under attack. She wiggled her foot at the ankle, pent-up energy struggling to find release in the back of the SUV.

Finally, they made it to the hotel. Hollis dropped them off with orders from Goldie to go back to get Tally.

Libby didn't want her friend to be alone, so she walked up to the lobby with Goldie.

Goldie approached the desk.

"My usual bungalow, thank you."

She didn't need to introduce herself. She probably never did anywhere on the planet.

"It will be just a moment, Ms. Hayes. Can we get you a drink?"

"Yes, vodka and soda, a double. My nerves are shot. Libby, you?"

"Yep, sounds good."

"We'll be by the pool."

"Yes, ma'am."

"I stayed here after I won the Oscar and after I broke up with Drake. It's a good hideout."

Libby knew there was quite a history to the place and was amazed at how sort of dingy it looked. But whatever, if Goldie felt safe, that was key.

It took less than two minutes for that safety to evaporate.

"GET GOLDIE GONE!!"

Libby and Goldie turned around to see another dozen Victor Universe t-shirted zombies working on getting past the hotel bellman.

"How in the heck did they know I was going to be here?" Goldie said.

"Get us out of here," Libby said to the desk clerk.

He was quick on his feet and escorted them to an office, away from the lobby.

"I'll be getting the police, so sorry about this, so sorry."

Libby and Goldie sat in the office of the hotel manager. Libby was stunned at everything that had transpired since she'd found Goldie's little dog trotting out of her gorgeous home.

"I'm at a loss. This is insane."

Goldie, for her part, also seemed stunned by the turn of events. Even in the life of a major movie star, the last few hours had been nuts.

"You didn't have this place on your schedule."

"No, they must have followed me."

"Unless..." Libby's suspicions had been raised back at the convention center.

A few clicks on Twitter, and there it was: an exclusive video of the crowd at Dream Factory Comic Con. There was a video of Goldie running. Someone had already sold the footage to the paparazzi.

"One of the fanboys?" Goldie asked.

"No, this is us running *toward* the camera. Look, the partition is behind us, and so is the crowd. It could only be one person."

"Hollis!"

"I'm afraid so."

"He sold the video and then tipped them off that I'd be here? He's worked for me for three years!"

"They were probably paying big money."

Goldie put her head in her hands. "Ugh, now what, now what?"

"You need to get out of L.A."

"I do. Yes."

"Come to Irish Hills with me. There's a flight at four."

Goldie looked at her.

"Lake Manitou? I mean, I do need to be really under the radar."

"No more under the radar than the old Two Lakes Grove Hotel. Remember that place. It's totally empty. You'd have the run of the place, and you'd have your Sandbar Sisters. We'll help you hide out. Lick your wounds. Drink. Whatever you need."

"I thought Hollis was a friend, sort of. I guess he was just here for the money."

Libby wanted to hug her friend. She wanted Goldie to feel safe enough to cry, yell, or do whatever she needed. But Goldie had a wall up; it had been up even before the events of the day. She was used to being taken advantage of by people wanting a piece of her and not giving anything in return.

Instead, Libby reached out a hand again. Goldie took it. Goldie blinked away tears. She squeezed Libby's hand in thanks. And then pulled back and wiped her face.

"Your idea is the best one on the table." Goldie fished her cell phone out of her purse.

Libby watched as Goldie dialed.

"Hey, yeah, it's a no go here. I'm getting out of town," Goldie said.

"Oh—" Libby whispered, "you need to tell her to meet us at John Wayne Airport. That's where we're flying out of."

"No, we're taking my Net Jet," Goldie said to Libby. "I'll reimburse you for your commercial ticket."

"What?"

"Kid, I haven't flown commercial since *Beautiful Girl* broke the box office in '92. Do you have luggage for Tally to get?" Goldie winked at her.

"Uh, it's in the rental car outside your house."

"Grab my friend's stuff out of the car, return it to, uh, John Wayne too, but later. The priority now is getting us out of here. Also, do not tell Hollis. He no longer works for me."

Well, okay. Libby watched as Goldie made one phone call in which half a dozen details were sorted.

"Also, send a car and driver to the Marmont. Get that going after the jet. Don't tell anyone anything. I'm going way under-cover. Make sure the wigs, the hat, all that is easy for me to get to. See you in Van Nuys."

Libby was flying a private jet back to Michigan with the biggest movie star in the world. This really was the weirdest day!

The good news was that Libby had succeeded in convincing Goldie Hayes, super famous superstar, to come back home to Irish Hills.

The bad news? They couldn't tell a soul.

Goldie

Libby was quiet as they landed at the small airport. It was a dark night now in Michigan. The day they'd had seemed as though it had lasted for a month.

Goldie appreciated Libby giving her space. And she was grateful to have a friend right now. She was so stung by Hollis. He knew her. She thought he respected her.

But he was in it for the buck, just like everyone in L.A.

Tally had arranged for a driver to meet them at the airport. That was Goldie's instruction, except when they got there, it was a rental car with no driver.

"Crap, this won't do."

The Net Jet flight attendant loaded her bags into the back of the SUV. Was this a Ford? She hadn't been in a Ford since her last time in Michigan. She smiled, seeing the logo. Her dad drove a Ford Bronco, and her first car was a used Ford Escort. Back when she used to drive.

"Didn't you tell Tally to pack two weeks' worth of clothes?" Libby asked.

"Yes, she obviously didn't listen."

"Ha, yeah, five bags is uh—"

"—Ridiculous, there's no way I have everything I need," Goldie said.

"Really? I was thinking you'd probably need one bag, if that, for a month here," Libby laughed.

"Well, anyway, who's going to drive?" Goldie said. "I haven't driven myself anywhere since Y2K."

"I got you."

Libby took charge again, getting behind the wheel. Goldie got in next to her. Libby really was a godsend right now.

Goldie was so impressed with her old friend. She had stepped in and protected Goldie. She'd seen the fans turn on her before Goldie sensed it.

Libby drove, first on a dark highway, with a little traffic, but not much. And then they pulled off the highway onto a rural state route.

Finally, they turned again on a country road. Goldie knew the roads, but thirty years was a long time. And it was dark, darker than L.A. ever got, even at midnight. There were always lights in L.A.

"Does it look the same?"

"Exactly. Though, there is still tornado damage. A lot of people picked up and left after that."

Goldie wasn't quite a townie—J.J. was the only true Irish Hills resident back in their day—but she was close. Goldie grew up in Tecumseh, Michigan. Her family owned a grand Victorian home on Chicago Boulevard. But they also owned a string of rental cottages on Lake Manitou. At the height of her parents' rental business, they owned eight on Cedar Point Beach.

The Libby family were founding homeowners in the area, but

so were the Goulds. Goldie's grandparents had the foresight to buy a stretch of beach and construct a row of small cottages. They all had names. There were The Poplars, The Sunnynook, The Cedars, and The Hickories. Goldie tried to remember all eight names, but they didn't come to her right then. Each cottage layout was the same: two bedrooms, one bathroom, an efficiency-style kitchen, and a back porch. That was it, but that was all that was needed for a vacation on the lake. The Gould family stayed in one each summer and managed the rest for renters. Sometimes they'd hop from week to week to whatever cottage was open.

While the Libbys came to live, the Goulds came to manage the rentals. Goldie spent most summer mornings doing whatever her dad said needed to be done for the cottage guests. And then he'd let her run wild for the rest of the day.

Every summer.

The cottages had been severely damaged in the tornado. Goldie thought back to that day when her dad explained how it was more financially prudent to get the insurance money and cash out.

And that was it. No more Lake Manitou summers. Though, to be honest. Goldie wasn't interested in being here or in Tecumseh or the Midwest by the time she was seventeen.

She knew she was headed for Hollywood by the time she was in first grade.

She was ready to go find her fame before her high school cap hit the ground at graduation. She was in such a hurry. Now, all she wanted was to slow things down a bit.

Libby insisted that Goldie stay with her at Nora House, owing to the late hour.

"I'm not dropping you off at the hotel in the middle of the night," Libby insisted. "But if you're up to it, I'll drive past it on the way."

Despite the hour, Goldie was awake. She had a lot to think about. Plans to make. But one thing was certain: she'd be hidden here. No one would suspect she'd high-tailed it from the Chateau Marmont to the middle of nowhere Midwest.

"It's just up there," Libby said.

Goldie pictured what all this looked like in daylight, but it was a thirty-year-old memory. Who knew what it looked like now, in what state?

"What do you remember about the big hotel?"

"Ice cream socials there? We also used to get renters to ask about it. I remember that. They'd go over to the slide. There was a big yard, beach, and shuffleboard, right?"

"You got it. Two Lakes Grove Hotel is no Chateau Marmont, but she's a grand dame! She could use someone like you who has a history here."

Goldie ignored the sales pitch. She wanted a hideout not to turn into Bob Newhart. What was that show where he had a hotel? Goldie's mind always reverted to TV and movies.

They drove off the main road and onto an offshoot that led to the hotel.

Despite the hour, the moonlight did its job. It reflected off the inky lake and gave a glow to the building Libby pointed out.

The hotel was there, it had to be one of the biggest structures on the lake, bigger even than Libby's Nora House, but Goldie remembered it as summery and elegant. She had no way to tell now, as they rolled up in the middle of the night.

Libby slowed down. Goldie could make out the outline of Two Lakes. She had an urge to get out, walk the huge lake-facing porch, explore the rooms, and just get lost in something that wasn't her career drama.

But Libby was right. It was night. They'd traveled a long way since the morning when her agent stabbed her in the back.

"I'm excited to get in there and explore." And she was. A hotel all to herself, with no fanboys or people trying to get pictures of her looking old in her swimsuit.

"You'll have total anonymity. Not a soul would suspect the world's biggest movie star was holed up at Two Lakes Grove."

"That sounds like Grey Gardens."

"Nonsense, you'll add life, not haunt it."

They turned from the road to a private drive and drove a mile. They didn't encounter another single vehicle.

Goldie strained to see more of the tree-lined lane that led to Nora House.

"How many times did I ride my bike up here?"

"Countless."

Goldie and Libby's history went back the farthest of the Sandbar Sisters. They had run around together as soon as they were old enough to drop training wheels. Their families had owned places here in what seemed like the "olden days" to both of them.

Nora House was a second home to Goldie. The drive curved in a familiar way. The dark tree cover opened up to the house and the darkly shimmering lake beyond.

"Wow, she's a beauty, even in the dark."

"Thank you. Aunt Emma was going to get me back here, one way or another, and once I got here, I was so angry with myself for forgetting how much I loved it."

"It was fun, those days," Goldie said. But she had no regrets leaving her small town roots for her big fancy life. No, not one bit.

But still, her heart felt warm, knowing she'd get a chance to revisit some of the good times here for a few days at least.

"Which one of these do you need?" Libby asked Goldie.

"Oh, yeah, sorry."

Goldie was used to bags appearing in her room. She was accustomed to linens being turned down and counters being wiped, all without her participation. This had been the case for decades now.

She sourced out the day-to-day chores of life to focus on her career. This career focus included maintaining the illusion of her appearance with workouts, facials, injections, and the occasional surgical tweak. She filled her days preparing for a role, performing the role, promoting the movie, or negotiating for the next role. Her nights were about charity events and proper sleep.

Getting her own bag from the back of a car? She had people for that. She wasn't ashamed of that. She had designed her life around her career. But here, now, it made her look a little silly.

Goldie grabbed the bag that had her casual clothing. They were packed to her specifications, so she knew which one contained her skin care, her supplements, and her other toiletries.

"Ah, well, if Tally did the packing right, this one would do. Casual attire is still *de rigueur* in Irish Hills?" Goldie asked.

"Quite. I'd loan you some cut-offs and a sweatshirt, but I'm twice your size."

"You're trim and model lanky. I wish I had your height. I swear those bro dude directors won't let me do action because I'm short. No amount of Botox can fix that situation."

"Do you want to do action?"

"No, but still, it's the principle."

Goldie gripped the two bags, and they walked into Nora House. Outdoor lanterns glowed, and a light was on in the foyer to guide them.

"Oh, Libby, it's so perfect."

"Thank you, Aunt Emma kept it up well. I have a lot to do, but saving Irish Hills is first; renovating this ancient kitchen is second."

"No, I love it just this way, the way we remember it."

"Well, the Wi-Fi is updated, so that's good if you need to check-in, or maybe it's best not to look for a day or so."

"Or ever again."

"It will blow over; this trending stuff comes in and goes out before you can blink."

"I hope."

"Meantime, I'll show you to your room."

They went through the beautiful main sitting room. Wall-to-wall windows made it easy to see how Libby's automotive mogul great-grandfather knew this was the best spot in the county for a house.

"I've got you at this end of the hall. You've got the use of this bathroom. I'm downstairs. Can I get you something to eat? Anything?"

"Libby, no, nothing else. I never eat at night. I'm rather exhausted. Do you mind if I just crash? The breeze seems lovely, and the room is perfect."

Though Goldie was hungry, she was used to feeling empty. Feeling empty meant she could fit into her wardrobe.

"Girlfriend, sleep. Sleep in. Tune out. Whatever you need. We'll go to the hotel tomorrow whenever you want."

"Okay, but I sort of want to go early. If that's okay. Before anyone around here is up and about."

If this was going to work, this hideout, she'd need to be in the secluded Two Lakes Grove Hotel before anyone could catch on.

"Sure, I get up early. I'll be ready when you are."

Libby reached out and gave Goldie's arm a squeeze. Libby was a hugger, Goldie knew, but she wasn't ready to let down her guard. In fact, once she got to Two Lakes, she would fortify the walls she had between her and the rest of the world. She'd think of it as a retreat or something. Meditate. Detox. Plan. It could work.

Libby padded downstairs and let Goldie settle in. The room was a throwback to the sixties of the Kennedy era. There was a wicker high-back chair in the corner and a tufted bedspread on the double bed. An ornate dresser, a mirror on one wall, and a little attached bathroom. Everything was neat and well cared for, just outdated, but somehow, Goldie was comforted by all the style, the era. She grew up in the eighties but with sixties décor all around her. She hoped Libby didn't overdo the makeovers of this house. It had a vibe that worked.

Goldie set up in the little bathroom and removed her makeup. She applied the ten different steps required to keep her skin exfoliated and hydrated. Finally, she collapsed onto the little bed. A double was tiny, really. But it was comfortable enough for Goldie to fall asleep. No Ambien, no cocktail, no melatonin, just the gentle breeze in the window, the lapping of the water on the dock outside, and the clean, cool sheets surrounding her did the trick.

Chapter Six

Goldie

They arrived at Two Lakes Grove Hotel early.

"The hotel comes with a campus, as you can see. And if you remember, the row of Gould cottages was just up there. It really was an adorable little resort corner here for vacationers."

Goldie remembered. When they all saw *Dirty Dancing*, Goldie envisioned the cottages, the hotel, Nora House, and even the dance pavilion as her own personal version of the movie. She was Baby, of course, but no one stepped up as Johnny. She didn't have a love story to remember from living in Irish Hills. The only love story she had, was on screen.

They got out of Libby's Jeep, and the air temperature was a bit of a shock.

Michigan, in July, could be hot. Goldie had forgotten that. She remembered freezing springs and socked in the snow in February. Sure, she spent warm summers here, but she forgot how hot it was then.

And it was going to be hot today. Not the dry, still heat of L.A. but a heavy heat, one that melted you a little.

Goldie's mother called humidity the air you could wear. She was right.

Goldie worked up a sweat as she and Libby transferred Goldie's bags. Goldie was starting to feel a little stupid for traveling with all this now that she had to move it herself.

That weasel Hollis selling videos of her to the tabloids. It was why she was determined not to hire an assistant here. Even though, right now, she would appreciate that a lot.

Libby listed the features and benefits of the Two Lakes.

"So, there are a dozen rooms, one main dining area, and a kitchen that needs work. Think about it, a return to hosting vacationers in Irish Hills! Just like your parents. On that note, Hope is willing to set up a breakfast delivery of pastries and whatnot for whoever takes this place over. Could be nice synergy."

"Ha, I think it is perfect for me to hide out. That's all I can do right now, you know?"

"Oh, I get it. Totally."

"I can't wait to see the girls."

"I was thinking drinks and dinner at Hope's Plate. You're going to love that."

"Oh, but I don't want to be recognized."

"I promise you, the folks at the restaurant will be oblivious."

"I really don't want—"

"It's okay. You know, you're right. We can do it at my place. But dinner might be a little later, sis."

Sis. Libby called her sis, and Goldie nearly cried. Right there, out of the blue. Where had that come from? She swallowed the shock of emotion. She turned to face the lake just behind the hotel. She didn't want Libby to see her.

She was raw right now. Raw got you hurt.

"That's great, perfect." She was an actress, and by golly, she would act like she was okay.

She knew these women had no idea the kind of scrutiny or the lightning-fast way word traveled when a movie star showed up some place unexpected. Daniel Radcliffe ate breakfast at a Bob Evans in Flint, and it made national news. Keanu Reeves had dinner in Flat Rock, and Twitter broke.

"Okay, let me show you around. In recent history, the previous owners couldn't make a go of it and were about to put it up for sale. Irish Hills has been falling into decline since we all ran the place. Anyway, the owners were ready to retire and were ripe for Stirling Stone to snap it up."

In their travels yesterday, Libby had described her recent victories over the billionaire, Stirling Stone. She'd stopped eminent domain votes or delayed them, at least. Her aunt had blocked Stone's attempts to buy everything in sight.

Libby described how Hope's restaurant was a key in helping turn the downtown area around. And just two weeks ago, they were awarded grant money to finish their renovations. Part of Goldie felt bad. She knew things were bad when she left, but it was hard to hear the details. Memories of her old stomping grounds were all good, all bathed in summer glow.

But Libby was on the case. Whatever cause she set her sights on was going to succeed. That was how she was as a kid; now, her old friend was in her full power. Too bad for Stirling Stone.

"Along with the guest rooms, four on three floors, there is a really nice space, off the main lobby sitting room. I think that's where we put you, come on."

Goldie looked around as she followed. There was carpet covering the floors. Who does that? She suspected there were wood floors underneath. The baseboards and molding were gigantic, another sign of an old home. No one built places like this anymore. The views of two lakes would be worth millions if this place was anywhere but Irish Hills.

But it needed work. That was clear. A lot of work.

"It's a fixer-upper, I am fully aware. We're slowly working on that. Whether I convince you that this is perfect for your investment or not, we're shoring it up. My aunt had plenty of plans, but the details of managing these properties, I guess that's why she needed me."

"I think your aunt is brilliant. I'd hire you to slay my dragons if I could."

"Don't tempt me. I'm so furious at your driver, at that director. But I know you'll be safe here, no one will know you're here, and the fanboys can stalk your place in Beverly Hills all they want."

"I appreciate it. Looks like the perfect place to set up my career strategizing command center."

Libby helped her unload her stuff in the manager's suite. Goldie was used to luxury, with every speck of dirt wiped away before she saw it. Unless she was on set; on set was a different scenario. She decided this was like the set of *Somewhere in Time*, with Jane Seymour and Christopher Reeve. Maybe he'd pop out of an old pocket watch if she was lucky.

"Look, I know you must plan your attack on the patriarchy. And I'm actually worried for the patriarchy. That said, there's a boat out there, a chair or two to lounge on, and other than the sound of outboard motors, it's pretty quiet here. Maybe consider giving yourself an actual rest. Just be careful by the water. The beach is overgrown."

"Thank you. This is a perfect hiding spot. People will expect me to be in Ibiza or the Amalfi Coast or The Hamptons."

"Yeah, true, but take this from someone who is just now learning how to relax. You look like you could use a bit of downtime wherever it is."

"I'd say we go over to the In and Out for live bait, find a tenspeed, bike around, and then, oh, what else, oh yeah, swim over to your raft?"

"YES! That's the summer right there!"

"I'm good here, thank you. I think more than anything else, I'll nap. And maybe put on some of the weight I took off to play in that superhero movie."

"I promise you Hope can help with that."

"Go on, you don't need to babysit me. I know you have stuff to do. Let the charms of the place work on me, and you work on your crusade to save the world."

"Well, this little corner. You sure you are okay?"

"Yes, I'm very Greta Garbo. *I want to be alone* is on my business cards."

Libby looked at her and cocked her head. "Call me, text me, send a heron if you need anything. There's one that thinks he owns this beach."

"Got it."

"I'll text you dinner details. You'll fall in love with this place. I guarantee it."

"Great, go, get out of here. You've done enough."

Libby left, and it was sweet how much her new old friend seemed worried about her. She hadn't been mothered in a long time. Goldie was also glad to just breathe, walk around this place, and not be noticed.

Goldie looked at her phone. A text from Tally. It was grim. The house, her salon, and her favorite lunch spot were all under siege from angry fans of the movie franchise she'd just destroyed. Please. She'd had one disagreement over one scene. And the director melts down?

The bottom line was he didn't want her in the movie. She stood up for herself, and he figured out how to use that to can her. And, in the process, bring down her career.

She didn't want to think about the deeper problems. Because there were deeper problems.

Goldie had sacrificed a lot, everything, for her career. That it could go up in flames so quickly was hard to process.

Though, if she really thought about it, it had gone up in little brush fires after she turned thirty and then a wildfire after forty. She wasn't fifty yet, and it was gone.

A check of Twitter revealed the hashtag #getgoldiegone was going strong.

The Wi-Fi here was spotty though. Maybe that was a sign to stop torturing herself.

Goldie found the correct bag, filled with her favorite piece of the line of athleisure wear that bore her name. Goldie Laps. That was a dumb name. She should have known that business was a bad idea based on that stupid name.

She did love the clothes, though. Thanks to an old friend, every garment she had lent her name to, she'd stand by today.

Goldie put on a pair of biking shorts and a tangerine t-shirt and tied a little jacket around her waist. Everything was color coordinated. She loved her athleisure line, but alas, Kate Hudson did it better.

Goldie found her walking shoes and decided to walk around a bit outside. She'd have days and nights to look around the hotel. But right now, the lake called to her.

She was used to the spectacular views of the Pacific. It had been a while since she'd seen the pastoral views of her summer haunts. L.A. was crispy in the summer. The foliage usually burnt out. Sure, there were gorgeous beaches and gorgeous people, and the ocean was divine. But there were brown trees and burnt grass a lot of the year.

Maybe she should get a place on the beach?

Goldie slathered on sunscreen and also donned a hat for extra protection. She'd spent a lot of money to keep wrinkles at bay; darned if she was going to let the sun damage what youth she had left.

She recalled days and days of unprotected sun worship here. Her current sunspots were directly attributed to this place, she realized. They used zinc oxide on their noses but only after the skin had bubbled. Wow, she really was dumb back then. Makeup artists had covered her nose freckles for decades; she blamed her Tecumseh Tan for that.

It was technically still morning, but barely. Goldie was on California time. She'd slept well, despite all the things she had to keep her up at night.

She walked around a bit on the main floor of the old Two Lakes Grove. The main lobby area, sitting area, and kitchen were gorgeous in this place. She took a peak in the main dining room. It was smaller than she remembered. If the hotel was at capacity, it would be tough to get them all in here at the same time.

But what did it matter? She was the only guest. Her old friend had given her a hotel, all to herself, where prying eyes could not find her.

That said, before she went outside, she applied her eyelashes, a light base coat, nude lipstick, and a dusting of blush. Even with all that, it was the least make-up she'd worn outside of her house in years.

She made her way out to the veranda facing the lake and, for a moment, stopped in her tracks.

The blue sky was reflected in the water, making Lake Manitou look like the Caribbean this midday in late July. At the corner of the porch, you could turn to see Round Lake. The two lakes looked more gorgeous than she remembered.

It may be blue right now, like the Caribbean, but there was a different sound to this lake as opposed to the ocean. The ocean roared some days. Other days, there was a steady hum. The sounds of the lake were its own, and today they were gentle. There wasn't a breeze right now, so the water was still. Small ripples rolled slowly across the surface.

It was calm, not imposing. Sometimes the ocean felt to Goldie as if it wanted to fight her. As if it wanted to swallow her up.

Suddenly, she realized why she didn't have a place on the beach in California. It was the fight. The strength of the ocean was so powerful it was just one more force she had to work against to get where she wanted. She'd fought for her career, contracts, and respect; at every turn, something powerful fought against it.

As she watched a pontoon boat slowly float across the water, she felt at ease in this place. Crickets chirping or a squirrel chittering was as intense as it got here. It also made her feel connected to her family, her parents, even though they'd moved away from here years before they'd passed.

Goldie wanted to get down to the water.

The staircase down to the hotel's beach was rickety. Goldie carefully made her way down to what was probably once a lovely lawn. Guests would lounge here, layout, play shuffleboard and badminton, and just sit and chat.

The hotel had been here when she was a kid, and now she wondered when it was built. Had her grandparents strolled around these grounds in the forties? She liked the idea. But she knew it was even older than that, more like turn of the last century.

Goldie got close to the water. There was no dock. And the lawn sort of just dissolved into the water. There was also not a beach to speak of.

Truth be told, it was a mess.

She decided to leave her shoes on. She remembered, back in the eighties, they had to wear swimming shoes on some of the beaches. Thanks to a hard-shelled invasive creature, what were they? Oh yeah, Zebra Mussels. The little suckers were everywhere and could cut the soles of your feet. They also served to filter water, which wound up cleaning the lake, but for a while, you had to be careful not to get shredded.

It didn't look like they were here anymore, but still, she spent three hundred dollars on her last pedi and had three more pairs of athletic shoes in her bags.

Better safe than sorry.

Goldie waded in; the cool water sluiced over her ankles. She got bolder and took a few more steps in. Before she knew it, she was up to her knees. Though, at her height, it wasn't that difficult to be up to her knees.

"Ew," Goldie realized too late that the bottom here wasn't sandy. It wasn't sand so much as muck.

Goldie took another step, and a slimy tendril of seaweed wrapped around her legs. She hated the sensation and lurched forward in an attempt to get it off her. What she managed to do instead was get further entangled. She tried to lift her foot and discovered that the muck had suctioned her shoes. The water was up to her thighs now.

"Great, after all this time, I'm going to die in quicksand."

Goldie got one foot free, but the other stuck, and she lost her balance.

All of a sudden, things were a tad more serious. She was chest deep, one foot trapped, and seaweed constricting her ability to do anything about it.

She swallowed a mouthful of lake water, and part of her brain did appreciate that it wasn't salty. The rest of her brain had determined that she was about to die and ramped her nervous system up accordingly.

Goldie flailed around, making the situation worse, and wondered if she'd get good media coverage when they found her body.

She wasn't so much being pulled under, as one would be in an ocean undertow, but rather sinking down, like the lake bottom decided she was a spaghetti noodle.

Goldie flailed her arms and swallowed more lake water.

Then a strong arm lifted her up, so she could stand again.

"What, ugh, who?"

She looked up to find a fully clothed man standing in front of her, trying to get her to calm down.

"Miss, miss, you're okay."

Ooh, he called her miss. Focus Goldie, focus.

"I got you."

"You do *not* got me. I'm drowning here. My feet, I can't get my feet out of the muck!"

"Miss, just hang on. The water isn't deep here, you—"

"Not deep? I'm barely five-two! It doesn't have to be!" Goldie barked.

"Miss, be still. You need to be still." He reached out and put his hands on Goldie's shoulders.

"Don't!" She was about to yell that he shouldn't touch her.

"I am going to hold on to you until you're calm."

Goldie was not calm. She was panicked, no question.

Goldie wanted to yell at this stranger who was ignoring her orders but was panicked, not stupid. She was stuck. And he was the only option at the moment. Even though she wasn't a fan of being told what to do.

She stopped trying to escape the muck. It wasn't getting her anywhere. That much was true. She took a breath and then coughed.

"You've got a heaping helping of lake water in there."

"You think I'm calm now, so let go. I need to get my feet unstuck."

"Do you have a plan for that?"

"I, ugh." She tugged her foot and proceeded to go under again.

The man pulled her up. He was only in waste deep while she was sinking.

"Now, unless you want to get sucked into the core of the earth, you'll do what I say, okay?"

"Fine."

"I'm going to go underwater; you keep a hand on my shoulder. And I'm going to get your feet out. You have shoes on, I saw. Won't take but a second."

"How did you know I have shoes on? Were you spying? Are you a pap?"

"Pap, no. Spying, no. But I saw a trespasser come down here, and it caught my eye. You can thank me later. Now. You ready?

None of this arm waggling. You'll make my job harder and get another gulp of lake water for the effort."

She wanted to argue that she was no trespasser, but Goldie was starting to be worried that she would, in fact, drown if she didn't listen to the big bossy stranger.

"Okay," she said. She put a hand on his shoulder as he instructed. It was all muscle. Well, that was good. He'd be able to carry her out of here if she did manage to pass out or some additional calamity. He smiled at her and then dove under the water.

She felt one shoe loosen and then the other. She stepped back with one, then the other foot and her big bossy stranger emerged again.

"Now, if you don't want to get that jam again, I suggest you swim, don't walk, back to land."

"But it's so... reedy."

"They won't kill ya unless you get your feet stuck in the muck here."

"I get it." Goldie swam back to shore and climbed up onto the weeds that hugged the little beach. She laid on the grass face down for a moment until the grass started to itch her bare legs.

"Miss, seriously, are you okay?"

Goldie flopped back over, sat up, and looked up.

"I am fine. But now that you mentioned trespassing, what the devil are you doing on this property? It seems to me you're the trespasser."

"Ha, well, you're welcome."

The man was soaking wet like she was. He ignored her as she stood up and tried to reclaim some semblance of dignity. She was used to having the upper hand with total strangers.

Instead of lending a hand to help her stand up, he pulled his wet t-shirt off. He was beefy, somewhat hairy, and sure there were muscles, but not of the Hollywood type, more of the functional type instead of the decorative ones that looked good in a superhero costume.

"Put your eyes back in your head, lady. It's rude to stare." He smiled at his own stupid joke.

"I am not staring; I've asked you a question you've yet to answer."

"Hmm, well, I'm not sure that's your best conversational gambit. 'Thank you for saving my prissy life' would probably serve you better around here."

He wrung out the t-shirt as he said it, barely giving her another glance.

"I'm from here, I'll have you know, and I'll ask again, or I'll call the police."

"From here, eh? So that question, what the devil am I doing on this property? Well, besides saving your life, I work here."

"The hotel is closed, so you're a trespassing liar."

"I've been hired to fix the million things wrong with Two Lakes so they can sell it. You can call Emma Ford or Dean Tucker if you'd like a reference."

"Well, kindly stop spying on me, whoever you are."

"You're a piece of work. Speaking of work, I'm going to get some dry clothes on and get back to it. I'll do that back at the house so as to avoid your leering gaze."

This jerk appeared to be thoroughly amused by what had been a very serious situation.

"My what?"

"Now, if you can make it up the hill without grievously injuring yourself, my name's Joe Cassidy, Cassidy Contracting, should you like to check my references."

"You can be sure I will."

"Oh, and you're welcome."

Goldie watched as he walked back up to the hotel. She did not leer, though. The shape of him was impressive. Which was why it was no big deal for him to haul her out of the muck.

Except, it was a big deal. And she had been in a spot.

Goldie decided to get the last word. "Thank you, Mr. Cassidy. I do appreciate your help."

That did it. He was shocked that she had done an about-face. That was her gift! She could disarm just about anyone if she really tried.

He turned around and flashed a smile at Goldie. He had a sexy smile and an impressive jawline. She loved impressive jaw lines.

"Now stop looking at my butt."

"I was—"

But before she could reply, he was around the side of the house.

Goldie hadn't got the last word, but she would have the last laugh. He may be ruggedly good-looking, but he was totally rude.

She was going to call Libby immediately to complain about this barbarian lurking around the property. And he better be telling the truth because she was going to check, boy was she ever.

"Ah! What's that?"

She felt something slimy in her sports bra. A strip of seaweed had slid in there, ew! She whipped out the offending vegetation and proceeded to do an involuntary dance of revulsion.

She'd check on that rude contractor later. First, she needed a shower. There was sand in every crevasse she had.

So much for rest and relaxation.

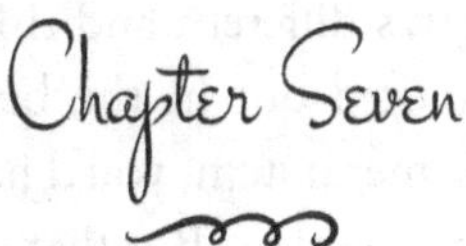

Chapter Seven

Libby

"So, we're a go with the Goldie Hayes Film Festival. What's the first step?" J. J. clapped her hands together and rubbed them like she was relishing the spectacular salad Hope had placed in front of them.

Libby had primed her two friends to start planning a big event. J.J. and Hope were eager to help. But they needed to pump the brakes.

"I don't think we can do that."

"Why?" J.J. said as she stabbed a forkful of Hope's lunch.

Hope, as usual, was behind her counter, and Libby and J.J. were at it, enjoying today's lunch offering. The deep green of the romaine lettuce contrasted with the bright red raspberries. The goat cheese from Windshadow Farm on top of it all distracted Libby for a moment.

"What's the dressing?"

"I made a sunflower seed vinaigrette. It'll be on the salads for the weekend's dinner service. You like?"

Libby didn't answer, as she was too busy chewing. Instead, she nodded. Hope's concept was working. Her friend asked guests to trust that she would give them the best plate of food one could procure in this little corner of the world, filled with the bounty available right here. It was different and risky. As Camila, Hope's restaurant manager pointed out in the beginning, if you had a hankering for a specific menu item, you'd have to wait until Hope deemed it ready to grace her plate. But that rarity made every plate, every bite, special.

Unfortunately, this gem her friend had created was hidden here in Irish Hills and getting the word out had proved tougher than Libby had anticipated.

They didn't have the luxury of a slow build.

That's where Goldie was supposed to come in, but now, that plan was in jeopardy. Libby reluctantly put her fork down and explained the situation to J.J. and Hope.

"Okay, so the film festival, we're not doing it? I thought that was the whole point of getting her here, aside from us getting to see her." J.J. was talking with her mouth full, and Libby fully supported it.

"Yes, that was the point, but she is in hiding, literally. The way I convinced her to come was to put her up in the hotel. It's secluded. It's got the woods on one side and the lake on two corners, so no one will be able to see that she's there. Well, unless they're floating by with binoculars. Oh, look, Earl, it's Oscar winner Goldie Hayes!" Libby was confident that she'd put Goldie in a good hiding place.

"Or, living in the caretaker cottage because you told Dean and me to get a guy."

"Oh, yeah, I'll have to give her a heads up. When's he coming?"

"Uh, Dean set him up yesterday. Joe's a great find. He's an expert in historic restoration, and also, he's a hunk. Anyway, he was about to take a job in Covert Pier. We had to move fast. He's back in this area to be close to his son and grandson."

"A hunk? We're how old?" Hope said.

"Never too old to appreciate a good-looking man, anyway. Dean said he's got a few weeks in between jobs, so he snapped him up."

"That's good." Libby was only slightly worried that Goldie would run into a hunky contractor on sight and flip out. She added it to today's list of worries.

"So, no film festival, what gives?" Hope didn't have time for tangents. Thankfully, she got the conversation back on track. Hope's success here depended on Libby figuring out how to get people to Irish Hills. Like Libby, she was motivated to make Irish Hills a happening little summer tourist town.

They had won a grant from the Small Business Downtown Revitalization Authority, but now, they needed traffic!

"She's been burned badly by her director and her agent. We practically ran out of L.A. with a pack of wild Victor Superhero Universe fans throwing tomatoes at her. Trust me, I've never seen anything like it. She's a pariah at the moment."

"Oh, that's awful. She's a goddess. What in the world?"

"Right now, she's in hiding, and that was the only way I could get her here. I mean, Irish Hills is very quiet, and the odds of being spotted by paparazzi here are, uh, well, let's say about as likely as being abducted by aliens."

"Ah, wrong, Herb Redding. He was abducted last year. Just ask him."

Libby narrowed her eyes at J.J., who appeared to be serious.

"What? It wasn't nearly as bad as when a sasquatch pulled Betty LaPierre out of her car through the driver's side window over on Addison Road. So, you know, just heads up if your windows are open."

Libby soldiered on and outlined how she'd gotten Goldie here. "Be that as it may, she's a no on a film festival. My Plan B was to make the news by having her eat here. We could be the downstate Traverse City with her celebrity. But it isn't going to work."

"Did you ask her?" Hope said.

"I asked her about the film festival and asked her to eat here, but it's a no-go. Now, I feel like the priority has to be whatever she needs," Libby said.

"Agreed. She was a Sandbar Sister long before she was an Oscar winner," J.J. said.

"I'm in full agreement as well, but we need to come up with a different idea, hopefully soon. The restaurant isn't anywhere near capacity. I'm in a position to have to lay off two servers less than a month into the operation."

"Ugh, yes, okay. I'll think of something." Libby didn't have the answer yet.

"We have to figure it out. This isn't all just you anymore. We're all in this," Hope said.

"Right! Now, you told Goldie, dinner at Nora House?" said J.J.

"Yes. I offered to pick her up, but she said no need." They'd all be there since Hope didn't serve dinner on Wednesdays. "Anyway, you bring this dressing, and we can't go wrong."

"Got it," Hope said.

Libby had defied the odds so far in Irish Hills. With Hope and J.J. on her team, she felt the odds were getting better daily.

They'd figure something out.

The priority with their friend Goldie was to reconnect. She needed to know she could trust them when she couldn't trust anyone else.

Libby wouldn't bother Goldie about the town's problems. She had enough of her own right now.

Chapter Eight

Goldie

Goldie showered, changed, discovered there was no laundry service, and started to question everything about this plan to hide in Irish Hills.

She needed to get her phone charged first off.

She had zero bars, and the battery thing was red. Normally, Tally did this, the tech stuff. Before Tally, there was her assistant Dylan, and before Dylan, it was Kara. She'd had a personal assistant going on twenty-five years. But a lot of good that did her while hiding out in Irish Hills.

The primary occupation of Goldie Hayes had been her occupation. She had someone for everything from laundry to technology to drive her where she needed to go.

She walked around the main floor of Two Lakes. She found an outlet in the main sitting room and plugged in her phone.

The view caught her attention. She marveled again at how pretty this spot was. With these rooms, a place this size, on water, could easily be ten million bucks somewhere chic.

But here, in the Midwest, who knew what real estate like this went for?

Goldie continued to explore the first floor. Off the kitchen, there was a huge pantry. The shelves contained a few food items. Did she need to buy food?

She decided against that. She'd order takeout or something. If she was going to stay much longer, maybe she'd look into getting a chef.

Scratch that. She wasn't staying long. This hideout was temporary. She could take care of her basic needs for a few days. It wasn't that she couldn't do things for herself. It was that she didn't have to. She had a pile of mucky clothes to launder while her phone charged. After that, start making some calls to find a new agent. You couldn't go it alone in L.A. without a shark on your side. She needed a shark.

To the left of the pantry, another door revealed a laundry room. It was large, old-fashioned looking, and smelled funny. Like bleach and Tide mixed in with mold. The appliances were harvest gold, actual harvest gold. In L.A., they'd call these vintage. Here, probably they were just old, but there were two washers and two dryers. They were probably doing a ton of laundry here back when they were booked solid.

"Okay! Now we're talking."

Goldie rounded up her sopping wet clothes from this morning and put them in the washer. At home, she did not operate her washer. All she knew was that it was a computer, just like everything else. There was a panel that controlled everything, and it looked like it could also launch the space shuttle.

"Ah, you're old school. Thank goodness."

Goldie put her clothes in, set the dial to small load, cold, and dropped in a cup of the nearby powdered detergent.

She hit start. And boom, one thing accomplished.

Back when she was a kid, it was her job to wash all the linens in the cottages. Sunday, they'd pick up all the linens, get the wash started, and she'd help her parents clean before the next set of guests would arrive. She remembered it was a quick turnaround.

She also remembered thinking, as a girl, that the moment she could hire a maid when she was famous and a movie star, that was the first thing she'd do. Movie stars didn't do laundry or change bed sheets!

Sure, if pressed, she could still make a crisp-looking bed.

But she was rarely pressed these days.

Goldie had hired a housekeeper first, and then a driver, and then an assistant.

Because of them, Goldie's home was meticulously cared for. She didn't have time for it. She had deals to make, hair to get electrified off, red carpets to walk, and lines to learn. Her priority was always her career.

Goldie walked back out to the sitting room and checked her phone. It wasn't fully charged, but there was enough to make the call.

"Auntie Goldie! Oh, my goodness, the news, it's nuts."

"Well, hello, are you sure you want to talk to the evil witch who brought down the Victor Superhero Universe?"

"I do. Mom and I have been worried about you."

"Tell your mom I'm fine. I'm in hiding. How is your mom?"

"You know, eyeballs deep in the color of the sky at dawn in July, in Montauk."

"Ah, sure, I know it well."

"She can get distracted by color palettes, and I'm like, hello! Can we get back to designing?"

"Ah, it's her process. I'm glad you're there to drive the bus when needed."

"So, hiding out. Is it that serious?"

"I had a water bottle come at me at a high rate of speed, and Trevor Sunday's minions are bent on making my life in L.A. miserable right now. But it will pass. They'll get over this movie delay and start obsessing about some other stupid thing."

"According to Twitter, you're unhinged, but those that love you know the truth. Never fear."

"Oh, except today, in my super-secret lair, I lost it completely when I ruined my best walking shoes."

"I hope it wasn't serious."

"They were five-hundred-dollar shoes!"

"So, very serious. Got it."

"Look, I just wanted to check-in. Tell your mom I'm good. I love you both."

"Love you too, Aunt Goldie."

"Good luck helping your mom capture the color of the sky at dawn."

"In Montauk, don't forget, the color is Montauk specific."

"Got it. Talk to you soon."

"Take care!"

Goldie hung up the phone. It was good to let them know she was okay; hiding out, yes, but okay.

Goldie sacrificed everything for her career, happily.

But one sacrifice had been the hardest, even though it had no doubt been the best.

Goldie
1999

By the last week of filming on *Tenured,* everyone on the crew had Oscar dreams in their heads.

From the very first day of shooting, the dailies were getting raves from the studio execs.

The movie was based on the book, and even the author had given thumbs up to the work they were doing. Goldie played the free spirit, the troubled young woman in need of a ride to California. Dustin Toms was the lead. He was playing the grizzled old professor who, after the death of his wife, embarks on a cross-country trip.

He gives Goldie's character a ride, and they fall into a romance. Dustin was playing older against his normal action star type. They'd let his hair go gray at the temples for this.

America was used to seeing Dustin Toms in a totally different way, but for *Tenured*, he would be a revelation. That's what the studio was saying. That was what Goldie could see each day they filmed.

Goldie and Dustin had chemistry, and it wasn't an act. The long shoot, in dozens of locations across the country, had pushed Dustin and Goldie together. There weren't any five-star hotels in South Dakota where they shot for ten days. They were in hotels, dive restaurants, and in the middle of nowhere, just like their two characters.

Eventually, the on screen chemistry turned into a kiss, and the kiss turned into a passionate affair.

It was a dangerous path, Goldie knew, but she found herself in love with Dustin Toms. The real Dustin, not the one the public knew.

They had a secret between them, and it made the scenes they filmed that much more electric. Her agent told her the studio was talking Oscar buzz for them both.

But Dustin Toms was married. Famously married. It was easy to forget in South Dakota, away from the spotlight. Heck, away from decent phone service. It was also easy for Dustin to minimize when Goldie expressed her worries.

The problem of Dustin's wife, an actress turned talk show host, wasn't a problem, Dustin insisted.

"It's been a sham for three years. She just doesn't want me to announce a divorce during sweeps, but it is over. It's just paper-work at this point."

The things you'll believe when you want them to be true. She believed Dustin. It was a piece of paper, a business arrangement between Dustin and his wife. Nothing more.

The location shoot had taken three months. The affair ignited almost immediately.

It had been an amazing experience. Creatively, Goldie knew she was turning into something more than the typical ingenue character. She knew Dustin was, too, bringing something special to this story. They were creating art. She felt it. This was the first time she believed that about one of her roles.

But the last week of shooting, the director commented on her figure. She was used to that in her business. This comment wasn't out of the ordinary, but it did get her thinking.

"Wow, your rack looks great in this. Wardrobe should have had this top for you the entire shoot."

Sexist comments were normal. She was a puppet, after all, in someone else's puppet show. That was the price of the job. The more famous she got, the more it appeared the directors wanted to be sure to show her she was nothing but a pretty face and hot body. No matter how high her star rose.

She could ignore comments easily enough. Really easily, since her career was going like gangbusters, and she was in love with a movie star she used to dream about as a kid.

It was her fantasies come to life on the set of *Tenured*.

But that comment about her chest did make her look at herself more closely in the full-length mirror of the wardrobe trailer.

She was decidedly bustier all of a sudden.

And then she did the math and realized why.

Her life was about to get one more glorious step toward a fairy tale come true!

She was going to have Dustin Tom's baby!

Goldie
Present Day

. . .

Goldie's walk down memory lane was interrupted by water all over the floor.

The area rug was soaked.

"What the heck?"

Then she heard the spraying. She made her way to the laundry room, and a hose was flinging around wildly as though it was a snake.

"Oh, man!"

Goldie put her hands up as the spray shot water directly into her face.

She screamed and tried to figure out what to do. What had she done wrong?

She opened her eyes, wiped the water from them, and took a step back from the laundry room. She had to fix this. The water was getting everywhere!

She backed another step up, right into the granite chest of Joe Cassidy.

"What have you done now, woman?"

"I didn't do anything; I was trying to do laundry."

Joe stepped around her, put a hand in front of his face, and turned the dial on the washing machine. It took a second, but the hose, previously animated with vicious intent, fell against the wall, limp and lifeless.

"Whoa, what a mess."

"I'll call housekeeping, ugh, I mean, I'll get—"

"Towels, we need a mop and towels."

"Mop?" Goldie was flustered, no question. She had temporarily forgotten there wasn't a staff or a manager to deal with the issue.

"Stick with absorbent fabric on the bottom."

"Ugh, I know what a mop is. I just don't know *where* a mop is."

As Joe continued to turn dials off, Goldie tried to turn on her heel and stomp off in a dramatic show of her annoyance. Instead, she slid on the soapy wet floor. She did not want to fall. But she was going down, no two ways about it.

Splat.

She was so embarrassed she'd have preferred to have died. She would rather have had a fall kill her than have to get up and face the infuriating Joe Cassidy, as he likely would laugh.

So far, Goldie had shown zero competence in their two encounters.

"Are you okay?"

"I'm fine, just fine." Goldie reached for the door jamb and, this time, got up slowly, with care.

She was soaking wet. Again.

"Wait, you're not fine."

Clearly, she wasn't fine. She was totally inept without Tally or Hollis. Ugh, Hollis.

"I am. Look, thanks for stopping the water."

"No, I mean you're bleeding."

Goldie reached up and put a hand to her face. She touched her eyebrow and looked at her fingers. They were bright red.

"Oh, no! My face! I cut my face."

"Let me see." Joe Cassidy got close again. This time he gently put his fingers on her chin and tilted her face.

"Is it bad?"

"It's okay. Why don't you sit down there at the kitchen counter? I'll grab a bandage. I've got a few in my toolbox."

"Bandage? I think I need a plastic surgeon."

"It's tiny, hidden there in your eyebrow."

This man had no idea how every little millimeter on her face had been tweaked, buffed, plucked, motion captured, and exfoliated. Over and over.

"You have no idea," she said. And then she touched her eyebrow again. It was tender.

"I do. This doesn't need stitches. It's a little scrape. Stay still."

He rifled through his giant toolbox, which was on the kitchen floor, and produced a bandage.

"I need to call my surgeon," Goldie said.

"Ugh, okay, well, for now, how about this?" Joe Cassidy deftly opened the wrapper of a tiny bandage. On it was a picture of Cromagnet.

"I can't get away from that guy," Goldie muttered under her breath.

"Ha, yeah, my grandson loves those Victor Superhero movies."

"Grandson?"

"Yeah, he's four, had a Cromagnet on his cake."

"Ah."

"Sorry, so what's your name?"

"You're serious?"

"I am. Maybe you did hit your head harder than we thought. Not too complicated a question."

"My name is Elizabeth Gould."

She was in hiding, and if this guy had no idea who she was, maybe it was so much the better. Though it was annoying. How did he not know who she was? VSU wins again. If you weren't in a superhero movie, your career was as good as dead. And if you impeded the superhero movie, well, you were the enemy.

"Well, Elizabeth, you're all set."

"Thank you, Mr. Cassidy."

"Call me Joe."

"Joe, thank you for helping me. I realize this is a mess."

"Yep, happy to. You seem to be accident prone."

"I'm not. I'm just off my game."

"Ah, okay, well. So far, you nearly drowned outside and inside. Maybe you need a lifejacket around your neck at all times."

"I appreciate your help. But I'm late."

For some reason, Joe Cassidy's smirk infuriated her.

"Sure, gotcha."

"And I'm going to be checking those references. I was told I would be alone here."

"Ha, okay, had you been alone, you'd probably be dead. But check away."

Joe Cassidy was done with her; he took his toolbox and gave her a strange look. "Don't use the laundry again until tomorrow. I have to replace that hose. It's old and corroded. That's why you had the disaster."

"Fine."

Despite his annoying personality, Goldie found herself staring as Joe Cassidy walked away.

This was the second time she'd caught herself doing that.

She shook it off. She did have plans. That was true. She was going to have dinner with three of her oldest friends.

Suddenly, she was nervous.

What if they didn't hit it off? What should she wear? Would they think she was inept, just like Joe the Toolman did?

Well, only one of those issues was really under her control. She walked back to the room she'd claimed. She opened one of her suitcases and selected her wardrobe for the night. Even this, figuring out what to wear, had been outsourced for her. In L.A., she had a stylist, a groomer, like a prized poodle, for any scenario where she'd be photographed.

Away from Hollywood, Goldie was coming face to face with the fact that all she knew was Hollywood.

The trappings of her fame had truly trapped her.

Chapter Nine

Goldie

She heard a whistle as she stood in the driveway of the hotel, the sun was setting, and the whistle was clearly a man, not a bird.

"Pardon me?"

"You clean up nice." There he was again, her new best friend. Also, somewhat cleaned up.

"You have no idea."

"The customary response to a compliment is thank you."

"Ah, well, thank you again. Seems like I'm racking up the thank yous with you, Joe Cassidy."

"Yes, well, I like to keep useful."

"You're sort of clean now, too. What's the occasion? The opera?"

"You're kind of a snob, aren't you?"

"Maybe," Goldie said. And she realized she was giving a hard-edged L.A. attitude in a soft corner of Michigan. She tried to let her guard down a bit.

"So, waiting for someone?"

"I'm unable to get the Uber app to open or get a car and driver out here."

"No Uber in Irish Hills and our limo services are abysmal."

"Of course." Goldie looked around. Now what? She had promised Libby she'd be there for dinner and not to worry about getting her there. Irish Hills was more backward than she'd realized. Getting a car was easy in just about every city on the planet.

"Can I take you somewhere? You know, on my way to the opera?"

"Stop, ugh, actually yes."

"Okay, get in the truck. Your eye looks like it's doing okay."

"Yes, I sent a picture to my plastic surgeon, and he agreed with you."

"You're kidding me, right?"

"No, I'm serious."

"Well, I guess it is good to get a second opinion. But with a face as pretty as yours, it's going to take a lot more than a little scrape to ugly you up."

"Thank you?" She had no idea what to make of Joe Cassidy's compliments. Or was he hitting on her?

"Where to?"

"Nora House, do you know where that is?"

"Sure do. Let's hit it."

Nora House wasn't far. She probably could have walked or rode a bike. If she stayed here, she'd have to arrange transportation.

"I appreciate it. I haven't driven in years."

"Really? You don't have a license?"

"No." She was going to elaborate but then realized how strange it must sound to someone from here that she had a driver, a cook, and a plastic surgeon, at her beck and call. "I used to drive. I used to like it." She remembered tooling around these very roads in her stick shift powder blue Volkswagen bug. She'd sold it to buy her ticket to L.A. and pay her first month's rent.

"Here we are," Joe said as they pulled out onto the road in his pickup.

"I think you have a bad impression of me."

"Nah, just a weird one."

"I'm really not this incompetent. In my real life, I get things done and have things done. I'm just going through, uh, well, something weird."

"No crime in that. Life can be a bear."

"Yeah, right now, yeah." She decided to change the subject. "So, just the one grandson?"

"Yeah, my son's boy. They both live in Tecumseh. Red has full custody, thank God, so I help out when I can."

Hmm. Goldie wondered what the story was there, of Red Cassidy and his son.

"I'm from Tecumseh."

"That is a shocking revelation if I ever heard one."

"No, it's true. Haven't been back in thirty, uh, a lot of years, but I'm from Tecumseh."

"Well, what do you know? I must have skimmed over that in your Wikipedia entry."

"What?"

"Yeah, I do recognize ya, Goldie Hayes. I didn't at first, by the lake, with the seaweed in your brassiere, not very Hollywood. But when you were fighting off the washing machine, I finally got it."

"Why didn't you say anything?"

"I suspect you have people recognizing you all the time. I thought I'd change it up for you."

Goldie was now worried this man would sell pictures of her, tip off the press, or tweet out her location.

"Look, I am in hiding right now. I've got a million fanboys out for blood. I was supposed to be in the next Victory Superhero movie, and it went badly."

"So how much is it worth, keeping that quiet?" Joe leaned back into the driver's seat and rested one hand on the wheel. He was casual as he considered how to milk Goldie's bank account. How lovely.

"I could do five thousand for the full week, and then an NDA, that would cover it."

They pulled into the private drive of Nora House. Joe stopped the car and looked at Goldie.

"I have no idea how things work out in L.A., but you're from here, it may have been a long time since you've been here, but we're not the kind of people who would sell pictures of a woman trying to take a few days off, to the highest bidder."

"That's because you just don't know the highest bid."

"I don't want money from you to be quiet. Your secret is safe with me."

Goldie sensed she'd insulted him, somehow. She was so used to the cutthroat world she'd been in for thirty years. She didn't know how to operate outside it.

"I don't even know you. How can I trust you?"

As soon as the question escaped her lips, a scream reached the truck from the direction of the back door of Nora House.

Goldie and Joe looked over to the source.

And there was J.J. Pawlak, running at top speed and screaming, "Malibu Barbie! She looks exactly the same!"

Goldie opened the truck door. She didn't think about it but out came, "Growing Up, Ginger, you haven't changed a bit!"

This was how they used to tease each other.

The two women were thick as thieves. They grew up together. They'd fought off her mother's crappy boyfriend. Goldie taught J.J.'s little brother how to kiss.

And it had been thirty years.

Goldie and J.J. embraced. J.J. lifted her off her feet! And soon, Libby joined the melee.

Goldie reached a hand out to Libby. She hadn't hugged Libby. She'd held back. She'd kept up that wall she had to have in public. J.J. had smashed it down in the space of two seconds.

Another woman followed Libby. She had a shock of white hair against thick waves of chestnut. She was striking. She looked like she took zero crap from anyone.

And then it clicked in Goldie's mind.

"Oh my gosh, Hope!"

Hope smiled, and her eyes sparkled like they did in Goldie's memory.

There were hugs all around now. Goldie had not earned this affection. She had not kept in touch with these women. They were really strangers. But here they all were. Together again, in the same place, with the same bond.

It was overwhelming, and Goldie thought she might cry.

For a moment, they all four stood there, without words, and held hands. What had their journeys been like?

Goldie was at a disadvantage. Her path was laid bare for the world to consume. They knew what had become of her. Though, they didn't know the details. They didn't know what it really took to make the dreams of Malibu Barbie real.

"Okay, let's take this reunion to the back porch. My cheese is melting," Hope said.

"That's menopause for you. Mine's always melting, even in February," J.J. added.

"J.J. spare this nice man the details of our hot flashes," Libby said.

"Oh, Joe, he's not a nice man. He's a rake, in the best possible way, of course," J.J. said.

"Oh, Joe! Yes, Dean was singing your praises. We need to talk. We have a lot to talk about." Libby broke up their little circle and zeroed in on Joe.

"See, I'm not a squatter," Joe said, winking at Goldie.

She rolled her eyes. She didn't really think he was, not after the washing machine rescue. But she was not going to admit she'd been wrong, dramatic, or totally ill-equipped to handle lake life.

What had happened to her? She used to manage the maintenance of half a dozen of her family's rentals. Now, she could barely wade into the lake, ankle deep.

"What? A squatter?" Libby said.

"I startled Ms. Hayes. From her perspective, I can see how if she's Malibu Barbie, I'm King Kong," Joe said.

Goldie rolled her eyes again.

This man annoyed her. That was it. He annoyed her.

"I'm sorry I didn't have a chance to introduce you and well, meet you myself."

"No harm done, right, Ms. Hayes?"

She sniffed in answer. He could have done a better job making it clear, and Goldie had decided not to give Joe Cassidy the satisfaction of anything.

"Okay, so you all head in. I'll touch base with Joe really quick here," Libby said. She turned her attention to Joe. J.J. and Hope turned their focus onto Goldie.

"We have so much to catch up on. Thank goodness I made a pitcher of green juice," J.J. said.

"Green juice?" Goldie asked.

"Don't ask, and also, don't drink it too fast," Hope said.

The two women guided Goldie up to Nora House.

Goldie took a sharp breath in.

"Oh, my gosh, it still looks so beautiful." There was simply not a better spot to see Lake Manitou than this wall of windows unless you were on that expansive lakeside porch.

"Right? Nora House doesn't disappoint," said Hope.

They proceeded out to the porch, and Goldie scanned the view for a moment.

"The pontoon, and oh my gosh! Our raft!"

"Right, Aunt Emma gave it all to Libby. She's making sure it's appointed to keep us floating and happy."

"Libby said you're a stylist."

"Please, I do hair. I do it well. Calling me a stylist is a little high tone for Irish Hills."

"Well, Libby's hair looks amazing, and I know you're the reason."

"True, true."

Hope added a dish of a creamy-looking dip to the center of crackers.

"And she tells me you own a restaurant here now."

"I do, Hope's Plate. We're small but mighty," Hope said.

Libby joined them.

"What did Joe say? How's it looking for the Two Lakes?"

"J.J., number one, thanks to Dean, we've got the hottest contractor I've ever seen working at that place," Libby said.

"Oh, I told him, only hire silver foxes with six packs. He listened, for once."

"You two are terrible," Hope said.

"Well, you've only got eyes for the neighbor boy," J.J. said.

"What now?" Goldie loved their easy banter. She wondered if she would be able to fit back in to keep up. Suddenly, she wanted nothing more than this.

"Oh yes, Hope bought one of the cottages at the end of Orchard Beach and Cottage Drive, and her neighbor is the town lawman."

"Lawman, you make it sound like we live in Deadwood."

Hope turned to Goldie and boxed out J.J. and Libby.

"Greg is a retired Detroit detective. The town hires him to freelance to keep an eye on the rampant crime."

"Crime's rampant?"

"Ha, no, that's why he likes it. He's got precious little to do, but make sure I don't get into a screaming match with my ex-husband."

"Oh, I'm so sorry."

"Don't be. We're happily divorced, or well, we're working on the happy part. It's all pretty new. Anyway, Greg is my neighbor, my friend. Don't listen to these two."

"Her neighbor who can't take his eyes off of her," J.J. said.

"And you're married to, uh, Dean, right?"

"Yep, he was a fixer-upper, but I've got him just the way I like him now," J.J. said.

"Don't listen to her now. Dean is the best man on the planet. Saved my plans a million times over with fixing up Irish Hills, and now with the hotel."

"On that, so Joe is there to do what, exactly?" Goldie was woefully under-informed. She'd flown here with one thought and that was to hide. Maybe get some rest after the stress of fighting the Hollywood machine while fitting into her super suit.

"Let's sit, have some food, some uh, green juice, and catch up on all of it." Libby was a consummate hostess. She was gracious, in control, and still looked like she'd be just as at home having lunch with the Queen of England as she did on waterskis.

"I have to admit, I am starving." Goldie didn't know how to cook. She didn't have her personal chef here and, in the last few days, had not eaten. She knew this was a cycle that could get her into trouble. It was one thing to blame the roles she had to play for skipping meals. It was another to let it be how she dealt with stress. Controlling the one thing she could, food, had messed with her health more than once.

Having a balanced attitude toward food was something she fought hard for, and it was precarious. Hope handed her a plate. It was an antique, clearly, probably from Aunt Emma's collection. Goldie began to fill the plate with the lovely crackers, the creamy dip, the cheeses, and a sprig of grapes.

"This is lovely, Hope."

"This woman is so talented; I mean, we used to be her sous chefs for cookie baking, but it did not wear off on me. I can't cook, not a lick. Well, I do mix a great cocktail. But that's a whole different skill set."

Goldie remembered taking Hope's orders in the kitchen, everything from lemonade to chocolate chip cookies.

Goldie sank her teeth into the cracker. The cheese melted in her mouth, and the seasoning was better than anything she'd sampled at the poshest places in Beverly Hills.

"Hope, this is sooo good."

A bit of cheese slopped out of the corner of her mouth. She quickly used her finger to pop it in. She didn't want to waste a morsel.

"Thank you, all local ingredients. That's my schtick."

"Wow, we've come a long way from Pop Tarts," Goldie said.

"But here we are, back again," J.J. said. "So, fill us in. You're a movie star, we all know you've dated just about every People's Sexy Man cover boy since the nineties, you have an Oscar, but in my opinion, you should have two. I got all the Goldie Hayes headlines, but fill us in."

"Two, eh?"

"Yes, *Tenured*, you should have been nominated for best actress, not supporting, and you should have won."

"Studio thought I had a better shot at supporting. Kim Basinger swooped in and won the thing."

"Yeah, I'm still bitter about it," J.J. said.

Goldie laughed. Most people in today's Hollywood weren't even born in 1999, much less remember her turn in *Tenured*.

"Kim was very sweet about it," Goldie said.

"But what about the real you? You keep that personal life locked up pretty tightly," Hope said.

"Yeah, most of what you see is made to order from my P.R. team. Heck, if I dated George Clooney, I don't remember it. But rumors that I did were enough to get me seen for a couple of big parts back in the early aughts."

"Well, who have you been in love with that we don't know about? The real Goldie didn't fall for anyone back in the day," J.J. said.

"Oh, I had a few pretty close calls at marriage but never really had the time to make that my priority. I'm wondering if I made a miscalculation. Here we all are, pushing fifty. My closest friend is an assistant I pay."

"Well, not anymore. You're a Sandbar Sister. We took a pause, a big one while we did big stuff, now we back, to whip this town into shape," Libby said.

"Here, here," Hope said.

They raised their glasses, filled with the potent green juice, which Goldie had come to realize, was a margarita 'a la J.J.

"To the Sandbar Sisters," J.J. said. "Minus, Viv, wherever she is right now!"

Goldie didn't have the right to tell some stories, or the courage to, quite yet.

There were sacrifices she'd made for her rise to fame that maybe her friends wouldn't easily understand. They all had husbands, ex-husbands, and kids. Goldie had an Oscar. That seemed like not quite enough.

"So, saving Irish Hills, what's the grand plan?"

"Have you ever heard of Stirling Stone?" J.J. asked.

"Oh yes, Libby mentioned him, her arch enemy. I actually have met him once or twice at events. Handsome devil, for sure."

"He's been pushing to buy everything. Aunt Emma stopped him, bought everything, paid folks' rent, I stopped him with eminent domain, and we all pulled tougher to win a grant for downtown improvement. He just keeps on ticking, though."

"What now?"

Libby hesitated and switched focus. It was easy to see there was something she wasn't telling Goldie.

"You know what, our job, right now, is to make sure the jackals don't get you. That's it. No pressure. No need to be on. No need to be Goldie Hayes. Just be."

"Thank you." She wanted to help them, she wanted to be a part of their enthusiasm for their little project, but right now, she needed to lie low. She needed to disappear.

"I heard you put the kibosh on a film festival. I was looking forward to finding a sequined gown," J.J. said.

Hope swatted her with a napkin.

Libby changed the subject.

"I'm sorry Joe's going to be there at Two Lakes at the same time you're there, but I do need to make sure it is ready for a buyer. Ha, unless you're interested. If I don't prove that we've got lovely accommodations here, Stirling's libel to put a strip club on Lake Manitou where the hotel used to be," Libby said.

"It's fine, it's really lovely, and I'm sure he will stay out of my way. And no, I really love the place, but you know," Goldie said. She suspected Joe liked getting in her way, but she wasn't going to complain to Libby. Libby was an adult. She didn't need Goldie acting like a child over nothing. That was a movie star tactic.

Libby's body language turned serious all of a sudden. And she looked Goldie in the eyes.

"Now, there's one more bit of old news we need to tell you about. It haunted me for decades. Just so you know, we did not kill Bruce."

"What? Who?"

"Bruce, my mom's abusive toadstool of a boyfriend. You know how we locked him out of Nora House during the tornado?"

J.J. explained, and it came back to Goldie, that moment they'd run down to the basement.

"Ha, you felt *bad*? Ladies! I haven't thought about that since the moment we came up out of the basement. Truly. What a waste of guilt!"

"I thought we legit murdered the guy," Libby said. "And Aunt Emma blackmailed me, more or less, to get me to help her save Irish Hills on the basis of that little moment."

"Wow, she's good. She would have fit right in Hollywood. Heck, I need a new shark agent. Maybe I should call Aunt Emma."

Goldie remembered the tornado, the destruction of the old

cottages her parents owned, but she hadn't shed one tear worrying about locking that dirtbag outside.

She barely remembered that. She had guilt, but it wasn't about that.

Her guilt was more personal. In her heart, she knew she did the right thing at a critical moment, so maybe it wasn't guilt she was feeling.

Maybe it was regret.

Chapter Ten

Goldie, 1999

For the first time in her career, Goldie wasn't withholding food from herself.

She was always counting calories, skipping meals, restricting fat grams, and bending over backward to keep her weight low.

But there was only a week left in the shoot, and they were done with the love scenes. Plus, Goldie was eating for two.

She hadn't told Dustin. She hadn't told anyone. But she was feeling great.

Dustin and Goldie had finished for the day. They had shot the last scene in the movie on the last day.

They'd done the movie in sequence, which she liked. The story on screen mirrored Dustin and Goldie's story off-screen.

She was ready to tell Dustin about the baby. He needed to know first. This kind of gossip could spread out of control quickly. It wasn't for the public. It was for her, the baby, and Dustin. Navigating it would be tricky. She knew that. But she believed they'd figure it out together.

Goldie knocked on the door to his trailer. They were in the middle of nowhere, on a rural road that had been shut down for their scene.

Everyone would soon be going their separate ways. A movie cast and crew really does become a tight-knit but temporary family. This time, it wouldn't be temporary. Goldie was set to fly back to L.A.

She wanted to tell Dustin here, on set, before the world and their real lives intruded. This was where they fell in love, and their little family began.

She knocked on the door lightly. Dustin opened it and nodded to her. He was on the phone.

"Yes, totally, we'll coordinate. Make sure you talk to Bernadette. Her schedule goes through Bernadette. Yeah, yeah, sounds good."

"Good phone call? You're smiling like you just got some good news."

"I did, I did. I'm glad you're here."

"I've got some good news, too," Goldie said.

"Great, great, so here's the thing. Laura is pregnant. Finally."

"Wait, I thought you two were not sleeping together. How is she pregnant?" Goldie also knew Laura Walker was a year older than Dustin and had a much talked about fertility struggle.

"We aren't, that was true. This is in vitro, I left my deposit in a cup. I honestly never thought this would work, but Laura has been like a dog with a bone. She just always wanted to be a mom."

"She *is* a mom; you have three kids."

"Stepmom, they're from my first marriage. Laura wants a baby of her own, wanted to be pregnant."

"Ah." Goldie's head was in a whirl.

Laura Walker, America's most popular morning chat show host, was pregnant, and Dustin was the father. She started to see the way this could potentially play out.

She was the other woman. Even though Dustin had assured

her his marriage was a business partnership that had run its course. No one would see that. He'd told her again and again how he would leave Laura now that Dustin and Goldie were in love.

Goldie realized with blinding clarity, so fast it nearly knocked her down that those were all just words. The facts were entirely different. She was the villain of this story.

Hollywood had not been kind to the other woman, no matter if she was a star or not. Elizabeth Taylor was pilloried, Ingrid Bergman roasted. She would be the home-wrecker even though she didn't make the first move. She'd resisted Dustin's advances. Until she didn't.

She was in love with Dustin, and he was in love with her. They shared chemistry, a connection. It was something special. Surely, they could figure this out. Whatever this was.

Goldie's brain felt fevered, like it was cycling through a million scenarios to find one that ended with her and Dustin and their baby together.

Dustin was pacing. He was excited. This was a different man than the one he'd been the last three months. The Dustin she knew looked her in the eye. Didn't hesitate to wrap his arms around her when they were alone in the trailer. He was attentive. It was intoxicating, to say the least, to have the world's biggest movie star make her feel like she was the only thing he cared about. But right now, he was barely talking to her. He was talking into the air. He appeared to be envisioning the press coverage he and Laura Walker were going to get.

"We're going to be interviewed by Barbara Walters. We're going to be on the cover of Vanity Fair. Laura is so excited. Oh, and once she starts to pop on the morning show, the fans will eat it up. Like *I Love Lucy* but real."

Goldie wanted to point out that Lucille Ball was real and actually pregnant on the show, too. But that was beside the point right now.

"What was this? You said your marriage was over. I mean, I wouldn't have fallen in love with you if I thought it wasn't."

Dustin stopped. He finally looked at Goldie. He turned his piercing eyes in her direction. He smiled, a smile that film critics compared to Clark Gable, a smile that she had been taken in by, a smile she thought was real. It was all an act.

"You would have fallen for me. Everyone does."

The smile evaporated. In its place was a clenched jaw. The eyes were cruel now. Who was this person? Goldie hadn't seen this side of Dustin, not once in their three months practically living together and working together every day.

"I—what are you saying? Spell it out."

"I'm saying that it made the movie better. You are in love with me for real. You're an okay actress, but not a great one, so I ensured that you didn't have to be a great actress."

The worlds coming out of Dustin's mouth were insulting, humiliating, and downright vicious.

"All this, what we were doing, it was an act?"

"You're actually asking me that?"

Goldie didn't answer. She felt stupid. She lashed out. "I'm sure your wife would classify what we did as real."

"Ha, well, this is the deal. She's pragmatic. She knows that her star is hitched to mine, and now with a baby on the way, well, even more so. Besides, she's about as monogamous as I am. You can go tell her or tell the papers, but you're going to look really bad. As a friend and someone who knows this business, I'm telling you, keep it quiet. You're on track for an Oscar nom for this movie. Don't blow it by being the other woman in America's Favorite Couple."

Goldie blinked away tears. She had been lied to. "You have no feelings for me, all the things you said to me," Goldie remembered promises, plans, confessions of love.

"I wasn't saying them. They were all my character."

"You're a monster!"

"Come on, save the drama for your next gig."

Goldie wanted to scratch his eyes out. She wanted to destroy his trailer. She wanted to destroy his career. She'd been a fool.

She'd come in here, ready to share her news.

She was so grateful for that one small thing that he'd gone first. She'd said nothing about the pregnancy.

"Congratulations on the baby." Goldie turned around and grabbed the door handle. The trailer smelled of cologne and whiskey, and it made her want to throw up.

"See you at the Oscars!"

She slammed the door behind her.

Goldie walked back to her trailer. She was in a panic. What in the world was she going to do now?

She was alone. Utterly alone.

Scratch that. She wasn't. She had a baby, too.

But what she needed right then was a friend.

Chapter Eleven

Libby Present Day

Not pressing Goldie was the right thing to do.

It was easy to see her old friend was wrung out. If she walked down the street, she'd be mobbed by fans and selfie seekers. But it appeared as if there wasn't a soul in the world who she could really count on.

She had climbed to the top in an absurdly competitive business. She'd made her dreams come true. The same dreams she'd declared to them as they floated on the lake all those years ago.

But the cost was high. Libby had her three kids and a budding romance with Keith. Hope had her girls. She, too, was finding great fun, dating at fifty! And J.J. was the center of Dean's world. They weren't mushy about it, but it proved a long-term marriage could be just as sweet as new love when she saw J.J. and Dean together.

Goldie didn't have any of those things. With her power and name, she somehow seemed the most vulnerable among them. She was almost adrift. Goldie Hayes didn't need a break on rent, a rich benefactor, or a free place to say. She had all that. But she needed real friends. Libby could be that for her. They all could.

Libby parked in a spot along Manitou Lake Road, the main drag of Irish Hills.

There were always available parking spots. Which was a sign of her current failure to lure tourists. Libby looked around. It was lunch. It was late July. This was just after the busy season on the lake. It was summer, for crying out loud, but there were only half a dozen diners at Hope's Plate. The place should be packed.

The sun was high in the sky. Boaters were enjoying all fifty-plus lakes that surrounded Irish Hills. Libby was so proud of the progress they'd made. But the buildings were empty.

The tourist dollar, which she'd sold Hope on and had convinced the town council she could produce, had not materialized.

There needed to be a reason to get all those summer tourists to Irish Hills. Goldie Hayes would have been a great counterpoint to Covert Pier's celebrity scene. Chef Rami Ellston was famous but no Oscar winner. His girlfriend, supermodel Mira Low, had major Instagram game, but still, Goldie blew them out of the water.

Alas, it was best for Goldie to be out of the public eye. Libby would figure something else out. She put Goldie out of her mind. This was solace, not social media, for her old friend.

She walked to the middle of the block.

These buildings were so darn cute now. Some businesses would be lucky to rent here. Dean had turned this dilapidated structure into the centerpiece of the stretch of buildings.

She unlocked the door and stepped into the largest rental space. The other two properties flanked it. This should be the star of the block.

Inside wood floors, high ceilings, exposed brick walls, and gorgeous lighting had turned the former General Store, and then Woolworths, into the perfect home for a new retail business to step in.

Libby flipped on the light switch and did a last look around.

Her finances were precarious. The grant they'd won had finished this part of the plan to fix up Irish Hills, but empty buildings were still empty buildings, even if the décor was pretty.

She would eventually get rent from Hope, that would help, but the restaurant was still upside down. Libby refused any suggestion that Hope pay her right now. That was not the bargain they'd struck. Libby had made promises, and she was dangerously close to breaking all of them.

Libby needed to start collecting rent on the other four spaces, or it would be back to the pawn shop with another piece of Aunt Emma's heirloom jewelry.

Her entire plan to prop up Irish Hills was unsustainable. Infusing cash into the town only made sense if it could stand up on its own and fast.

For today's meeting, she was prepared to do her best sales pitch. If she could secure this tenant, the major tenant for the block, they'd be in a better position.

Libby looked at her phone. It was ten minutes past noon, and the meeting was at noon.

She decided to call.

Darren Schneider picked up on the second ring.

"Did we get our wires crossed?" Libby asked.

"Actually, no, I'm so sorry, my assistant was supposed to reach out. I'm not going to be able to make it."

This was not good. This was terrible, in fact.

"That's okay. We can pick another time for a walk-through. I think you'll find that it's really the perfect spot to open. It's an emerging location and—"

"I have to stop you. We've decided on a space in Covert Pier."

"Oh, are you sure? Without even a visit, I fear you're missing out on a great opportunity to be in on the ground floor of what we're doing here in Irish Hills."

"I appreciate it, I do, but the bottom line is foot traffic. You have none. Our business model requires foot traffic."

"You're part of our incentive to get that foot traffic. Everyone loves Archeologie Stores. Your plan to open outlets in small towns; it's just brilliant and tailor-made for this location."

"We need numbers before we commit. To be honest, having a big name is what lured us to Covert Pier. Chef Ellston's home decor store, next to our outfitter outlet, was a no-brainer for us. His celebrity brand is powerful and growing. The town is bursting with tourists before we even get there."

"Let me guess, you heard about Covert Pier from Stirling Stone?"

"Yes, coincidentally, our CEO and Mr. Stone were golfing, and he mentioned Covert Pier. It sort of snowballed from there. It was really meant to be."

Meant to be? Right, meant to be. Libby tried to keep the sarcasm out of her voice as they finished the phone call. She didn't want to burn any bridges. No had turned into yes more than once in her career.

"Oh, gotcha, sure. Well, congratulations, and welcome to Michigan. If something changes, you know we'd be thrilled to reopen the discussions."

Libby had done all the work to identify the perfect tenant for the space, she'd called in favors to get in front of the decision-makers, and she'd ensured that the spot they were offering met the specs for the company's plan for outlet versions of their retail locations. She'd put together a pitch in record time. Today she was going to seal the deal. She was going to get an Archeologie Outlet in downtown Irish Hills. A great restaurant and fantastic discount shopping would be a perfect lure for tourists here, even in the off-season.

But Stirling Stone had done it again, swooped in, hobnobbed with his rich guy network, and squished her like a bug.

She walked to the window and looked out onto the sidewalks.

No one was there, not one person.

And why would they be there? There was nothing to do in downtown Irish Hills but look at empty buildings.

She banged her head on the windowpane.

July was slipping away. They were in the height of the summer.

And yet, her little resort town was as empty as the day she'd driven down the street in April. It was just prettier now.

If she didn't get people to Irish Hills, all the work they'd done would be for nothing.

And if she didn't start getting rent money for all the places her aunt had rescued, she'd be down to nothing as well.

Chapter Twelve

Goldie Present Day

Goldie woke up thinking about the laughter she's shared with Hope, J.J., and Libby the night before.

She pulled on her leggings, her tank, her sports bra, and the second pair of athletic shoes she'd packed. Thank goodness she'd packed four pairs.

Kids today called her style "extra." But Goldie was always this way. She always traveled like she was a movie star.

Of the Sandbar Sisters, outsiders would say Goldie's dreams were the most outlandish. She always knew she wanted to be a movie star. Growing up, adults told her it was silly. That her dreams were a little girl's dream, like saying you wanted to be a Disney Princess.

But she wasn't ever silly about it. She was single-minded. And her dream of being a movie star matured as she did. She wanted to be an actress.

She gave up everything else to make those things real.

The number of things that had to align to get her to where she was were almost uncountable. It started with genetics. Something completely out of her control. She had pretty parents.

At her house in L.A., she had a wall of mirrors in a closet that was bigger than this entire room. She'd had an automated dry cleaning rack installed too. Her clothes traveled up and down, and the rows would shift back to front so she could see what she had. When people visited, it was her closet that they remarked on. More than the zero-depth pool or the million-dollar artwork. Take that, Carrie Bradshaw.

The mirrors were there, not so she could admire herself, but so she could assess herself unflinchingly. She could see where sagging, wrinkling, or thickening was cropping up. She dieted, exercised, sucked out, or melted off anything that offended the camera lens.

Here, she had one mirror. Goldie couldn't get the full 360-degree view of the flaws she needed to eradicate. She ate a lot of food last night and probably had too much wine. Goldie meticulously calibrated her food, hydration, and supplements to fight every aspect of the natural progression of aging. Last night was not on plan. Not by a mile.

She'd started with those genes, nothing else. She got to Hollywood, and people thought she looked like Cheryl Ladd. When she walked into the L.A. casting director's office at eighteen, they met with her, thanks to her face, not her talent. The first job that earned Goldie her union card was a bit part, playing Cheryl Ladd's daughter in the tv movie, *Get Away From My Kids*. She had two lines, but that was enough.

Genetics wasn't everything. She'd pushed the producer of *Get Away From My Kids* to consider her for his next project, a pilot that didn't get picked up. But it got her seen, and then from that, she got an audition for the indie that established a buzz.

But it wasn't just her doing. Mitchell Ozock had seen something in her as well.

He'd guided her away from a Warren Beatty picture that was the biggest box office disaster of the year. (Kid, if you're good in it, no one cares; it's Warren's picture, if you're bad in it, this turkey will be all your fault.) Ozock helped make sure she was the only one the director of *Beautiful Girls* wanted for his movie.

Genetics, the right agent, determination, and then talent. She had it. But she didn't take it for granted. She wasn't a product of prestigious acting schools out east, but she did take classes. Acting coach Michelle Danner helped her discover how to approach a part and opened up a world beyond just memorizing lines or being cute. As she earned money, she invested in personal acting coaches. They were just as important to her as Pilates instructors.

Casting directors had to like you, directors had to see their vision through you, editors had to make sure your best cuts made it to the final product, and on and on before it even got to the public.

Finally, the audience, they had to see something in you. They had to root for you. They had to believe you were their movie star. They had to be connected to you. And that was intangible. It was unlearnable. It just was, or it wasn't.

Her career was a combination of all of those things.

But no amount of genetic luck could stop a ticking clock.

She was feeling weird. The amount of warmth, enjoyment, and just plain fun she'd had sitting with her old friends, made her a little panicked. Goldie had blinders on her life, that's what made her successful, but this morning it was dawning on her how much she'd blocked out with those blinders. She'd carefully blocked the very things that made life worth living.

It was too late to change course now. She was only here to hide and figure out how to handle the blowback from the fanboy outrage.

It was great to see the girls, but she needed to get her focus back, her drive to succeed in Hollywood. Because you didn't just luck into that part, you took the luck and beat it into submission.

Goldie found her phone. She needed to get her agent situation figured out. That was job one. She had been dropped by Scott

Ozock. Ozock Group was the biggest game in town, for sure, but not the only game.

It was early in L.A., but she didn't care.

Agents would be happy to have her on their roster. One she'd been eyeing in particular. She dialed the personal cell of the agent, who she thought might be the answer to her current career dilemma.

"Hedda, it's Goldie Hayes. How are you?"

"Ha, I'm fine, but I bet you're not. This town is not happy with you right now."

"Really, I wouldn't know. I'm scouting new projects out of town."

"Don't B.S. me, I know Ozock dropped you."

"Please, I dropped him."

Perception was everything in Hollywood, and she was perceived as poison right now, apparently. The truth was relative, so she needed Hedda to think she was the dumper, not the dump-ee.

"Right, well, you're side of the story is not the story right now. Look, you know I've tried to lure you over here before, but not under these circumstances."

"Well, since I dropped Ozock, I'm looking for a new situation. I've got several options, but I didn't want to leave you out." She had zero options, but the way to get work or an agent was to pretend you already had too much of both.

"Look, you know, and I know you're a huge name. One of the most talented actresses of your generation. But right now, well, you're poison."

"Honey, this is not the way to get me in bed with you," Goldie replied, speaking in the vernacular of her business.

"I'd love to have you on our roster. You'd be the biggest name on it. But right now, you're mud. The VSU won't work with you. Not to mention the little social media storm you're in the middle of with the fanboys."

"If you're really serious about wanting to work with me, give me a plan. Show me you're the right place to be."

Goldie was trying to Vulcan Mind Meld Hedda. Maybe a little cognitive dissonance would work to get her a new agent? She would make Hedda work for her before the woman even knew she was doing it.

"My first advice is to stay hidden. You're not going to win if you talk to the press. They're out for blood. You'll look desperate. Make them wonder where you are. Let 'em chew on it. You're a mystery. You're someone who doesn't care if the gaping maw of the Victor Superhero Universe is trying to chew you up. Let 'em choke on it. That, my dear, would be badass."

"I'll consider your idea. I'll let you know if I'm interested in your offer." She knew darn well there was no offer.

"Here's what I will offer. A little spying. Let me see if I can find out how your dailies looked. Maybe there's something salvageable. How strong can that current picture be if all it takes to bring down one of their tent pole movies is little ole you?"

"I'm tougher than I look."

"That I have no doubt about."

"Talk to you soon."

"Be like Garbo."

Goldie hung up the phone.

Her next call was to Tally.

"Tally, I need you to send me a car."

"What, to the airport? You're coming back? That's great, but don't come to the house. Picketers actually threw an egg at me when I drove in the other day."

Goldie had planned to send for a car, book the jet, and get back to L.A. to fight.

But Hedda's advice rang in her ears. And now Tally had warned that the fanboys were still stalking her house.

Her instinct was to go back to Hollywood. She knew how to be seen in the right places. She knew how to make meetings happen. Well, she used to. Mitchell Ozock had done a lot of that; they'd made a good team. Now that she didn't have him, she realized how much he had helped ensure that she made the right steps.

Hedda's advice of staying hidden had to be wrong. Goldie was going back. Tally could arrange the travel. She'd pound the pavement like she had when she was an unknown.

"Tally, why don't you forward me any important emails, scripts, requests for appearances, interviews, all that?" She'd say yes to a few events. Goldie would work the whole, *be famous for being famous* thing, just until she was back where she needed to be.

Tally was her gatekeeper. She managed the hundreds of messages that came in. Tally knew what to regard as important and what to politely decline. Goldie would reconsider some appearances that she'd poo-pooed a few weeks ago. Just to get the ball rolling.

"Well, there are dozens of interview requests, all regarding the Victor thing."

"And?"

"Uh, there are cancelations."

"I usually have a dozen script backlog."

"Yeah, some have been withdrawn. I didn't even know you could do that."

"I guess you can."

Goldie wasn't entirely convinced by Hedda's idea that she stay out of town, stay hidden. She wanted to fight back and clear her name. But the dearth of messages, requests, scripts, and the like made her see the wisdom of Hedda's advice.

The only thing anyone in Hollywood wanted Goldie Hayes for right now was to roast her over an open pit.

"Forget the messages. Put an out-of-office reply in everything, tell 'em I'm traveling, on an extended trip, and you'll answer only urgent requests."

"Got it. Do you still need the car?"

"Forget the car. For now. Put Myrna on the phone."

Goldie heard the soft snerfle sound of Myrna breathing into Tally's smart phone.

"Hello darling, I miss you. I love you!"

Myrna barked in response.

"She totally recognizes your voice."

"Thank you, Tally. Make sure she gets her nighttime treat."

She ended the call.

She walked into the sitting room lobby, walked back to the kitchen, and then in a circle around the main floor. She was pacing.

Goldie processed the information from Hedda and Tally. She'd avoided the gossip sites and social media. The image of the angry horde of superhero fans was nightmare fuel, but she hadn't really allowed herself to think about the long-term situation.

All she'd worked for really was gone, at least right now.

She'd always been in demand. And now she was, what did Hedda say? Oh yeah, her name was mud.

Having an open schedule was weird, and it made her antsy. Having no plan past the very next hour, was not her natural state.

Goldie felt jittery. She was unmoored in every sense. As she stood in the middle of the room, looking at the expanse of the lake, she watched a blue heron skim the surface near the unkempt beach. She had no idea how to be herself in this nothingness.

But the view was pretty. She focused on it a few minutes more. She stopped pacing. She took a deep breath. Goldie couldn't honestly say she was confident that she'd figure all this out. But at least she had calmed her jitters. At least she'd stopped pacing.

Twenty years of yoga classes apparently did more that tone muscles. They helped her be in the moment, be in this moment. What came next was unknowable.

She heard a car pull into the parking lot of the Two Lakes Grove Hotel.

She walked to the kitchen service entrance and looked out. It was Joe Cassidy's Cassidy Contractors pickup truck. The white truck was muddy, the simple black logo slightly obscured by dirt. He needed to wash it.

Goldie watched Joe for a moment. He was good-looking; she'd give him that. He was strong and unkempt in a way no one in California was. You didn't just groom yourself in California. You hired a professional groomer. Just like a dog groomer here, she supposed. But fifty times as expensive. Joe's touch of scruffy was sexy.

She snapped out of that line of thought. She didn't need to fill the sudden quiet in her life with a totally ridiculous love affair.

Goldie watched as he started to unload his truck. As a distraction, more than anything else, she decided to greet him and find out what was on the plan for the place today.

She hoped he wasn't going to need her to get out of the way. If he did, she'd have no clue how to do that.

"Hello, looks like you've got big plans for the day."

"Yeah, late start too. Jared didn't have all the cans mixed yet."

"I love that Lil Pudding owns the hardware store now."

"What?"

"That's what we used to call him back in the day."

"Ha, I forget you've got roots here, Hollywood."

She brushed off the comment and watched as he made three trips with paint cans, drop cloths, and a ladder. Goldie's curiosity got the better of her.

"What room are you painting?" She followed Joe into the hotel.

"Main room, just white. Rooms all need it too, but big project first."

"Hmm." Goldie looked at the room. White was fine in the main spaces, she decided. "What about the carpet?"

"I'm removing that after the paint. Less tarp to worry about that way."

"Ah." Out of curiosity, Goldie went to the far corner of the room. She tugged at the carpet. Joe continued to busy himself with setting up for the painting project.

"Anything interesting?"

"Oh, my goodness, yes, it's original, I think."

Under the burgundy floral pattern carpet was wood plank flooring. The planks were narrow and dried out, but Goldie could imagine what they looked like back in their heyday before she was even born.

"This is gorgeous, it needs restoration, but it's *gorgeous*. Once this hideous carpet is off, you'll be able to sand it, refinish, heck, even match what's here, but you're under no circumstances to cover this with a carpet. Whoever did it the first time should be arrested."

"I'd love to restore the whole place, but Libby isn't made of money. Dean said that with all she's got on her plate, she's strapped pretty thin for cash."

"Hmm." Goldie hadn't thought too much about the financial strain her friend was in. She knew they were working to bring the town to life but hadn't considered what that cost Libby.

Goldie thought back to her fantasy about this hotel. She remembered wondering what it would be like to run this grand hotel instead of all the little cottages they managed.

She turned her attention back to Joe.

"White works, in here, but each room should be different, a theme, each one a place that transports the guests to a different place in Michigan, or many different eras? Or an homage to the old cottage rows on Lake Manitou." Her imagination was fired up now with ideas.

Goldie walked behind the front desk counter. There was an old reservation book. She opened it. Four rooms on each floor and an attic suite. The grand dining room was set up for family-style dining. It was suited for a bed-and-breakfast, she'd decided. Not a restaurant as it had been in different eras. They could have continental breakfast available and packed lunches, but then that was it. Let the guests go to Hope's Plate. Or over to Brooklyn.

She'd been staying in the manager's quarters and hadn't taken the time to really explore.

"Are all the rooms open?"

"Ah, yeah, wide open. Trying to get the musty smell out."

"Thanks."

Goldie wandered upstairs. Each room had a private bathroom with a shower/tub combo.

She wandered in and out. The smell of fresh paint wafted into the hallways.

Goldie's mind filled with the memory of the old cottages. Clean towels, fresh linens, and lake breezes, that was the selling point.

In one room, a TV on a stand sat, collecting dust. She ran a finger over the dusty thing.

"No televisions. Nope, not for Two Lakes. If you're bored at the lake, you're doing it wrong."

That was her dad's old saying. She said it as though it were her decision to remove TVs. She wondered if there was an old TV antenna stuck to the side of the building. That would have to come down if there. The plans started to form in her mind, and they didn't stop.

Each room wouldn't celebrate a region. They'd celebrate local lakes. Lake Manitou, Crystal, Devil's, Vineyard. She'd make each room a little nod to the biggest lakes in Irish Hills. She thought botanical prints of the native plants would be a pretty option for the walls. She could name some after the old cottages. Where could she find a list? She wasn't a decorator but had done so many houses over the years. Some of it had rubbed off. And she liked to think she knew what was tasteful.

"I think you've got company," Joe said, interrupting her thoughts of how she would run Two Lakes.

Goldie walked to the main door. Was it paparazzo? Was it a fanboy who'd finally found her?

She had no makeup on, was dressed in workout gear—not

even her best workout gear—and her hair was a mess. She could not be photographed this way. That was not how to gin up interest in her as a leading lady!

A tiny old woman was helped out of a car by a man in a business suit. They looked pretty formal for Irish Hills. The woman had a lovely posture. She wore a pretty pink sweater over her shoulders and a white blouse, with tailored pants and sensible shoes. It all looked rather expensive, actually. As they approached the house, it dawned on her that the woman looked familiar.

She flung open the door.

"Aunt Emma!"

"Oh, goodness, don't scare me like that. I'm on nitro, but let's not push the limits of pharmacology!"

"So sorry, here, come in."

"Well, now don't you look smooth as a baby's backside!" Aunt Emma said, and the two embraced.

"You know it's all fake, all of it."

Aunt Emma whispered in her ear, "Don't worry, I won't blow your cover."

"Thanks."

"But I want you to know I've seen every single one of your movies. Oh, except *Obsessed Attraction*. You're naked a lot in that one, I heard, so I just didn't think my lady's group would appreciate that. Talk about massive heart attacks left and right."

"Aunt Emma, you look beautiful. I have missed you." Goldie remembered Aunt Emma as kind of glamorous for Irish Hills. She still seemed fancy, lake fancy, if that was a thing.

"I'm glad you finally came home. It's been too long."

"Yes, that's true."

"Oh, and I heard you were the only one who had their head on straight about that Bubba situation during the tornado."

"Oh, yeah, not a concern."

"Exactly."

The man with Aunt Emma cleared his throat, and she turned and introduced him.

"This is uh, Tate, Tate Patrick. He's interested in buying the hotel. He's only in town for a short while, and I promised him I'd show him around."

"Oh, I didn't know."

"I meant to tell Libby to give you a heads up. Hmm, I must have forgotten. Happens, I'm four thousand years old."

Though she claimed to be ancient, and Goldie knew Aunt Emma was in her nineties, Aunt Emma did not seem to be over sixty in dexterity or when it came to her rapier wit.

"It's your place. I totally understand."

The man, Tate Patrick, looked at Goldie, and she knew he was figuring things out. Oh no, this could blow her cover.

"You look a lot like Goldie Hayes," the man said as he looked at her with a bit of confusion.

She lowered her sunglasses from her head to her eyes to try to throw him off track. "I get that a lot."

"You're clearly way younger," the man said.

Great, so she looked old on film. That's the takeaway. Fans also liked to say she looked skinnier in person. What did that mean? Ugh.

Aunt Emma guided the prospective buyer away from Goldie. They walked into the lobby. Joe nodded but continued to prep the space for paint.

Goldie found herself listening to Aunt Emma's sales pitch. Income potential, historic architecture, emerging area, lake access, and on and on.

"You know, Stirling Stone wants it too, but I think we need a more discerning owner here, don't you think, Mr. Patrick?"

"I do, quite right."

Aunt Emma walked out onto the back veranda, and Mr. Patrick followed. Goldie continued to hover just outside of the tour. But she was inching closer and closer to the discussion.

"I'm thinking we can turn this space into additional rentals," said the older man.

"What? Mess with this lobby?"

"It's all about maximizing income opportunities. You know I have a supplier for builder-grade bathroom vanities and old hotel TV armoires. It would be pretty cost-effective."

"Oh, and the carpet is terrible. I've got indoor outdoor in bulk. For a lake hotel, it's a must," Patrick said.

Aunt Emma, who'd mentioned historic architecture, didn't disagree with his garish plan to put crappy carpet all over the place.

"Look, if you buy it instead of that Vegas schlock peddler, you can turn this into a commune for all I care!" Aunt Emma winked at Goldie.

"The price is right. I mean, if your niece fails to turn the town around, I suppose I can flip the hotel."

Aunt Emma narrowed her eyes at the man. But it was clear he wanted the place, and he wanted to ruin it, in Goldie's opinion.

"I'll take it. If you can go down to three-fifty, I'll take it."

That was a low-ball offer, but Aunt Emma looked excited; she was going to take it. She clapped her hands.

Emma Ford was going to let this dufus put in indoor outdoor carpet, Wi-Fi, crappy fixtures, and who knows what else to take the charm out of the Two Lakes.

Goldie knew Libby and her aunt were cash strapped. She knew that she needed to sell. She also knew that Stirling Stone was the enemy. Aunt Emma and Libby would likely lose everything rather than sell to Stone. But in Goldie's eyes, this was no solution.

She'd already said no to this idea of buying a hotel, but that was before she saw it again. That was before her career prospects had dwindled to jack and squat.

Goldie made a snap decision. She stepped forward. She would not allow this place to go into the hands of this man, this Mr. Patrick.

"Aunt Emma, I'll give you four hundred thousand no contingencies, all cash. Today."

"Honey, that's quite nice. But Mr. Patrick was first in line, as it were."

"I really see the potential here to earn income, make this a nice little motel spot. I hear you can rent rooms by the hour." Mr. Patrick winked at Aunt Emma, and Goldie thought she might want to punch the weirdo in the nose.

"Ah, I think they call them no-tell motels," Aunt Emma quipped, winking back.

"Aunt Emma, that's—no! Okay, whatever. But I can assure you if you care about making this place lovely and bringing it up to the standard of Nora House, well, that's me."

"Oh, my, you sound like you have thought a lot about this. This is exciting. And boy, did my niece read you wrong."

"No, she didn't. I didn't have plans. Oh heck, maybe I do. Whatever I do, they do not include indoor outdoor carpet. If you want to bring life back to Irish Hills, the Two Lakes Grove Hotel is important. It needs to be returned to the showpiece it once was."

"And you want to do that?"

"I do unless you have a counter, Mr.—what was your name?"

"Tate, Patrick Tate, I mean Tate Patrick." He looked confused by his own name for a moment. He shook his head.

"Unless you have a counter, Tate Patrick, I'll get you the money today, and we have a deal."

"I'll match, four hundred."

"Fine, make it an even five hundred thousand." Goldie was not going to lose. She'd pay a million if she needed to.

"I won't be able to match, not that fast."

Aha! Goldie was victorious!

"I'll arrange a transfer of funds. You'll have them by the end of the day."

Aunt Emma and Goldie said their goodbyes, and the good buy Tate Patrick thought he was going to get was now hers.

Goldie stood in the center of the hotel she now owned.

She was exhilarated, filled with ideas, and excited to get started. In the entire time she'd been focusing on the hotel, she'd not once worried about her Hollywood career, or bro dude director Trevor Sunday, or causing wrinkle lines because it had been six weeks since her last filler appointment.

She was thinking a mile a minute, but none of it was causing her to feel sick to her stomach.

She owned the Two Lakes Grove Hotel. Or was about to.

Joe walked into the lobby. It distracted her from her mental celebrations and plans for the space.

"I did it. It's mine."

"This place?"

"Yes, I just bought it. That man was going to do tacky, tacky things to it. Or turn it into a place where you pay by the hour."

"Ah, romantic." Joe waggled his eyebrows at Goldie.

She waived her hand in dismissal. "This is supposed to be for family summer weekends, for maybe a wedding venue, or a family reunion."

Hollywood could wait a few more days. Maybe this was the answer. Maybe distracting herself from the mess of her career was exactly what she needed.

At least, for now.

Goldie tried to remember if she'd ever made a business decision that had nothing to do with movies or endorsements. She'd just bought a hotel because she liked it. Because it was a good distraction. Because she didn't want someone else to.

"Not to be a wet blanket, but do you have experience running a hotel?"

"Ah, kind of. I helped run a dozen cottages with my dad back in the day. I'm not totally inexperienced. I have stayed in a million resorts, the best in the country, the world. I know what they need."

"Ah, well, okay, I guess you're about to be the boss. So on that note, there's a raccoon in the attic."

"What?"

"Yeah, heard some scratching. You'll need to help me trap it."

"I'll need to what? Raccoon?"

"A girl who was born and raised in Tecumseh certainly knows what a raccoon is."

"I do, but trap it?"

"If we don't, it will eat your roof, and it will move its entire family in."

"Oh no! Okay, okay. We can't call someone?"

"Nope, not that I am aware of."

"Okay, so what do we need?"

"A trap, that's key to the trap plan."

"We're not going to hurt him or her, are we?"

"No, we'll get the little fluffy menace, and then I know a guy who will take him or her out to the country and release it."

"Okay, so trap, where do I go for that?"

"To the hardware store, Batman."

"Got it, I have a few calls to make, but I'll go with you. I need to take charge."

"Got it... and congratulations."

"Oh, yeah, Thanks."

Goldie was holding on to the high of coming out victorious in negotiations. The fact that she had to trap a wild animal couldn't bring her down.

Hollywood was full of wild animals, and she'd survived that. How bad could a raccoon in the attic really be?

Joe drove them to town, and she realized this was the perfect cover. The perfect reason to stay away from L.A. She'd do exactly as Hedda advised. She'd kill time here; she'd distract herself with this project.

And then, when the time was right, she'd make her triumphant return!

Chapter Thirteen

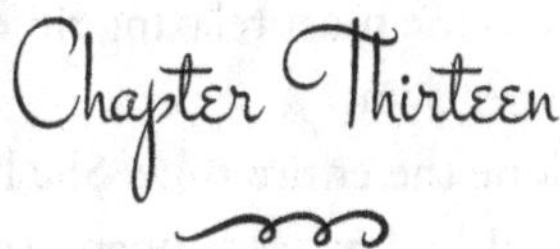

Goldie, 2000

The timing was tight.

By the time she'd finished all the filming, looping, and reshoots for *Tenured,* she was four months along. She needed to get out of town before someone other than a key grip who liked big boobs noticed.

She stayed at a rental house in Malibu as she watched Dustin Toms and his wife bask in the adoration of their lovely marriage and blessed news.

Everyone loved them. *Vanity Fair, People, Time,* and *Entertainment Weekly* all featured the two on the cover.

Mitchell Ozock was the only one who knew Goldie's secret.

"You'll finish it out in Europe. No one will care in Tuscany, trust me. We'll tell the press you're reading scripts, weighing the next phase of your career."

Goldie did just that. She rented an entire villa. No one could access the place. It was set way back, and if you wanted a picture of Goldie Hayes, you'd need a helicopter.

There couldn't be a more beautiful place to hide. The grounds were like living in a fairy tale. Goldie ate, took long walks among olive trees, she slept on the porch. She stayed away from prying eyes.

In some ways, it was the most relaxing time of her life, hiding a pregnancy in Italy on her own.

But she wasn't alone the entire time. She had reached out to a friend. And that friend had arrived, open arms, open heart, and ready to change both of their lives.

Her friend had tried to get pregnant for the last three years. Her friend wanted a family more than anything else. Her friend was married and had a successful business, but it didn't consume her life.

Goldie and her friend hatched a plan as Goldie prepared to hatch a human.

Her friend was there for six weeks. She was a godsend. She helped in any way she could. She'd get her a glass of water, lend her a hand as she strained to stand up from the grips of a squishy sofa and provided calm support.

The plan was unorthodox, Goldie knew, but it would work.

Goldie's friend would take the child and adopt it. She was also open to letting Goldie be the beloved aunt, extra mom, or whatever Goldie wished.

But Goldie knew she wasn't ready to be a mom, wasn't ready to explain to the world who the father was. Wasn't ready.

Goldie's daughter came into the world under the glow of a Tuscan sky. Her first moments were greeted with love from Goldie and from the mother, Goldie had chosen for this precious soul. A private doctor and staff, arranged by Mitchell Ozock, attended to her needs.

It was an easy pregnancy and easier delivery. Seeing her baby for the first time, Goldie decided that she wasn't the type who could just hand over her daughter and close the book. Goldie's friend did not pressure her. It was all easy, natural. It was right.

Goldie spent a month watching her friend bond with the child as Goldie healed from the birth. She needed to look like Goldie Hayes, movie star, when she returned to Hollywood.

But a month was all the time she could afford to give. She had to return to her career or see it vanish.

Goldie named the baby Siena, after the nearby village.

When Goldie was very pregnant and had let her hair get dark, under the cover of a big floppy hat, she'd walked the streets of Siena. No one recognized her, and she was charmed by each cobblestone step of the place. Siena was all good things.

She was Siena's mother. But slowly, she decided to settle into being Siena's beloved aunt.

Goldie kissed Siena's sweet head goodbye. There were tears when they all prepared to part.

Goldie, Siena, and Siena's chosen parents all lived in a beautiful bubble for a time. But it was time to go back to her real life. Having this baby was never the plan.

Having someone to care about, care for, and worry after, was new to Goldie. In the end, she knew this about herself, that she could provide all the things this child needed but couldn't protect her from the prying eyes. If anyone got wind of how sweet Siena came to be, she'd be the illegitimate baby that ruined Dustin Toms' perfect life. That was not what Goldie wanted for her beautiful daughter. So, they decided Siena would always know that Auntie Goldie was her biological mother, but Goldie would be Auntie. It would work. It had to.

"You're sure. You can change your mind."

"No one can know, and because of your open heart, I know this is the right thing. She'll have a lovely life with you. As long as you let me be the fairy godmother movie star that showers her with pixie dust."

"Of course, I never dreamed I could be so lucky."

"Same."

They hugged, with the sweet baby between them. Goldie's

good friend was now Siena's mom and her husband, Siena's new dad. They were a new kind of family. Their own kind.

"I'm going to be really crazy busy for the first few months, but then, maybe in the summer?"

"Whenever, always. However, she's your daughter, too."

"Auntie Goldie is just fine. I'm fine with it, okay?"

"Okay."

They secured little Siena in her car seat. The new family of three drove off. Goldie watched the car go. It was the first time her baby was physically so far from her. She would get used to it.

She flew home in a private jet, and another week went by. Hair, makeup, OptiFast shakes, wardrobe, meetings, scripts. It all came back into her life at a pace that was faster now that *Tenured* was about to premiere.

The film was a critical and commercial success.

Goldie was nominated for a SAG Award, a Golden Globe, and a Critic's Award.

She'd come back from Italy, and its relaxed clock, its luxurious pace, to the frenzy of her career. There was one more nomination that she coveted. The big one and it was the last one to announce.

It was early when the phone rang. She'd forgotten how early this happened because they liked to announce live on the morning shows that aired on the East Coast.

"Congratulations, you're nominated. Best Supporting."

It was Mitchel Ozock on the other end.

"Great, Dustin too?"

"Yeah, best actor, best director, best-adapted screenplay, and you. Now get skinnier. You've got a lot of red carpets to walk."

She'd be photographed a million times for awards season.

Goldie rose to the challenge of it. Only two months after having a baby, every inch of her was photographed. There was some speculation that she'd had a boob job.

She was photographed in her designer gowns. She was on

everyone's best-dressed list for every red carpet she walked. Even Joan Rivers praised her looks at each event.

"I'm not worthy," said the acerbic comedian when she saw Goldie on Oscar night.

This all fit the plan. This was Goldie's career leveling up, shining in a way she dreamed of when she was a kid.

Dustin Toms and his wife were lovely on the red carpet. They all posed for pictures. Press praised Laura for her post-baby body. She was writing a fitness book on how to bounce back.

Of course, Dustin won, and the screenplay for *Tenured* also won, but it had not been Goldie's year. She lost to Kim Basinger.

When the parties and press died down after the Oscars, Goldie curled up on her couch and opened the thick package that had arrived that day.

She poured through the pictures of baby Siena.

It had made the Oscar loss insignificant.

But it also fired a kernel of bitterness in her gut. For the first time, a sacrifice she made for her career was too much. She'd given up the day-to-day life with her daughter, for her career, and for Dustin's reputation.

He won the Oscar, had his wife, new baby, the love of the entire world, and a quiet and compliant former mistress and costar.

She could have unhinged his entire life. Instead, she'd quietly unhinged her own.

She was proud of herself, in one way, at least. Siena wasn't going to be a part of someone else's scandal. She was a beautiful light in the world, and Goldie was going to be sure that was always what she was, not some footnote to the story of Dustin Toms or even Goldie Hayes.

She would call tomorrow, at a better hour, and catch up.

She would bring clothes and toys and treats as many times as she could manage throughout the year.

She would be the best aunt she could be.

Despite losing the Oscar that year, Goldie had gained a lot, more than most.

Even if she didn't get the daily joy of seeing Siena, she'd figure out how to have the best of both worlds... or a little part of the best.

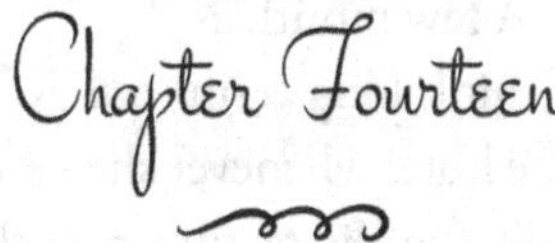 Chapter Fourteen

Goldie, Present Day

Joe drove, and Goldie got on her phone on the way to town. In less than ten minutes, she had the funds transferred where she needed them.

Aunt Emma and Libby would get a decent windfall, and Goldie would get a hotel! More than that, she had a valid reason to stay away from Hollywood while the scandal blew over.

"That's some wheeling and dealing," Joe whistled. He was amazed at Goldie, and maybe now he'd stop thinking she was an airhead actress. She had earned a fortune and could spend it whenever she wanted.

"Not really. I sort of know real estate. That's one of the things I invested my earnings in."

"Smart."

Goldie focused on the task at hand. She found it helped her stop obsessing about her career.

"Raccoon trap, what else do we need at the hardware store?"

"You're going to need a new hose for that washer. My fix was temporary at best. I'll install it, but we need to get it if you want to keep washing clothes."

"Yeah, I will need that." Goldie thought about her luggage, what she had, and what she needed. How long did she need to hide out? A couple weeks? A few months?

She didn't really think long term. Surely, she could farm out the management of the hotel whenever she needed to. But for now, she was happy to have the distraction and the project. She had rescued the place from tacky, that was the truth, and she'd helped sweet Aunt Emma. Libby, too, she hoped.

Joe handed her a washer hose, and she followed as he grabbed a metal contraption, the raccoon trap.

They made their way to the counter, where a good-looking man in a Peck's Hardware polo shirt helped check them out. Goldie knew right away who this man was!

"Little Pudding, you're a hunk!"

A bright red blush rolled from Jared Pawlak's neck to his cheeks.

"I didn't think you'd recognize me."

"Of course I do!" Goldie thought back to the days he tagged along. He was a pest!

"You guys were brutal. Remember the time you made me be all the boy parts for the backyard production of *Grease*?"

"I do. You were a great Danny."

"Ugh."

Joe was smiling. She half thought he didn't believe she was from here. Goldie supposed she came off as some sort of Hollywood Monster.

She was glad that Jared was making a fuss. She was happy to see him, and it was another sweet memory of her time here. She had wanted to get out so badly, get to her life, that she sometimes forgot that she started out pretty great, right here.

They chatted a bit, Jared explained the finer points of humane raccoon re-homing, and she made a promise that all her renovation supplies would be handled right here.

There were a few other customers in the store.

"We'll let you get back to your work. Thank you, Jared. We all set, Joe?"

"Yes, boss."

"Stop."

"Yes, Goldie."

They hauled their purchases out of Peck's, past a few customers who were now lined up at the checkout.

One customer had a t-shirt that Goldie recognized.

It was only later that she realized why.

Chapter Fifteen

Libby

"Why do you look so, I don't know, satisfied?"

"Well, I solved our cash flow problem."

"What? You didn't sell some diamond that was on the Titanic or something, did you?"

Libby, J.J., and Aunt Emma were eating lunch, as usual, at the perpetually empty but always delicious Hope's Plate. And sadly, Hope had plenty of time to pop into the conversation.

Libby tried to remember her line of questioning with Aunt Emma, but artichoke dip was melting in her mouth.

"Hope, this is divine. Wow. Okay, back to you, ya sly fox, what about selling Two Lakes?"

"Goldie's taken it. Patrick did the paperwork. You'll see, it's off your books, significantly over asking price!"

"What?"

"Yeah, you'll have to sign something or other, but it's off your plate. Goldie's on it!"

Libby hadn't seen Goldie yesterday, but today they all planned to get together for dinner.

"Wow, that's a change. I wonder what she's thinking?"

"Irish Hills beats Beverly Hills. We knew the old town had it in her," J.J. said.

"Yeah, but, wow."

Libby was amazed, and it was one less financial worry. If Goldie was handling the hotel, well, Libby could deal with a million other issues on the front burner. And a cash infusion, maybe she could start renovating across the street. She cycled through her list of projects.

Speaking of burners...

"You're going to make it tonight, right?" Libby asked Hope.

"Yep, I'll load up with leftovers; goodness knows we had them from service last night. Bad enough that we're not doing dinner again until Saturday night."

Libby hated to hear this. Her friend had worked so hard to make the perfect place. Libby had watched her blossom. But now, it could whither if Libby didn't get her end of the deal settled.

"I promise, it's priority one."

"So, no luck on our rental idea for the space next door?" J.J. said.

"No, but what about you do J.J's salon on the other end, Sandbar Sisters on each end of the block? It's perfect."

Libby was trying to get J.J. to break away from Hairdo or Dye and open a place of her own.

"If her frosted cupcakes don't get butts in the seats, my frosted tips won't."

"Fair point."

As they ate, they hashed out ideas to increase foot traffic, and they talked about possible ways to get *Food Magazine* to do a feature on Hope's Plate. All were good ideas, but none of them were as good as Chef Remi in Covert Pier.

As they talked, a group of diners entered. It was late in the lunch service. But it was nice to see.

"Hey, maybe the word is getting out?" J.J. gave Hope the thumbs up.

Hope left the group and got to work serving the surprise influx of guests.

They finished their meals, Patrick picked up Aunt Emma, J.J. headed back to the salon, and Libby was left to puzzle out her latest conundrum.

She left Hope to answer questions about her unique menu.

Libby stepped out onto the sidewalk and noticed more traffic than usual.

Maybe this was working. Maybe in increments, people were taking a little ride to Irish Hills.

She noticed cars parking in the spots along Green Street. She saw people walking, looking around, and taking pictures.

It was great. Goldie had decided to buy the hotel, for whatever reason, and there were tourists trying Hope's restaurant. It was okay. It was all going to be okay.

She decided to head back to the little office space she was using over the proposed mercantile space.

How did Traverse City become a hot spot? How did Waco? She knew how it happened for Covert Pier. It was the will and might of a billionaire.

What it came down to was they needed a big splash. Sure, they could slowly build, but they needed that film festival idea, or a food festival or a fair if they were going to bring folks in. Thanks to Aunt Emma's leveraging everything they owned, they needed a fast fix, not a slow build. Though it was nice to have Goldie's infusion of cash. She knew Goldie didn't want to be the town spokesperson, but investment from someone so high profile couldn't hurt.

Libby made a dozen calls. She was pitching the Irish Hills as hard as she could. But maybe, this was all too fast.

In reality, she'd moved here, pushed back Stirling Stone, and renovated the retail space in a matter of months.

She looked out the window at the street below.

Her phone rang. It was J.J.

"I think we have a problem."

"Yeah, what?"

"Take a look at the new foot traffic. Notice anything?"

Libby clocked a group milling around the hardware store and others by the grocery store. The original group was now coming out of the restaurant.

"Wait, they all have superheroes on their t-shirts."

"Yep. Wait, I'm getting a call from Jared. Hang on."

"'K."

"Uh, Jared told me Goldie was at the hardware store. She was with Joe; they bought stuff and mentioned the old hotel. They may have found her."

"Okay, well, stand by. I'm going to figure out how to throw them off the scent. We can't have them bothering her. I don't want a repeat of that Comic Con thing or the whack jobs at her house. If they figure out that she's there at the hotel, it will be miserable for her. I'll text you in a minute."

"'K, I'm over here on red alert."

"Tell Hope, too."

They hung up. Libby got on social media. She looked for the hashtag GetGoldieGone, and sure enough, there were pictures of downtown Irish Hills. Local fanboys were doing TikTok live in the restaurant. They were driving around downtown and on the prowl for Goldie.

Libby closed her laptop. She packed up her stuff and ran down to her Jeep. She speed dialed J.J. and then Keith.

If they were going to help Goldie right now, it would need to be all hands on deck.

* * *

Goldie

Goldie had to admit that she was having fun. It turned out she liked painting, talking with Joe, and hashing out ideas for Two Lakes.

Joe listened to her as she talked about anything that came to mind. He opened up a little about his son and his grandson. Part of the reason he'd come back to this part of Michigan was for them. Goldie learned that the tough contractor had a very squishy inside when it came to talking about his grandson.

And for a moment, Goldie thought maybe actually staying here wouldn't be the worst thing. But then she reminded herself there was retribution to be had against Trevor for trashing her career.

But an afternoon spent with Joe turned out to be a good way to forget about her career dilemma. Even for a little while.

Joe wanted to continue to work while Goldie got ready for dinner with her friends. She showered and spent more time than she anticipated scrubbing paint off her hands. She'd officially not been this dirty since the time they threw her in a vat of mud for the last scene of *Rancher Wife*.

She was excited to have dinner with the girls. To kick back and also to tell them about her ideas for the hotel. Libby, Hope, and J.J. were incredible. And the amount of time she had missed out on their lives, well, it made her a little sad. That was time she'd never get back. She'd always thought of time as her enemy when it came to her looks. Maybe it wasn't about that at all.

Goldie blew out her hair and did her face for the first time since she'd come back to Irish Hills. She entered the lobby to find a paint-covered Joe, finally ending his day as well.

"Wow, that's a fancy get-up for Irish Hills."

"Too much?" She was questioning her outfit choice all of a sudden. Was she showing off? It was so casual here; she didn't want to seem like she was too big for Irish Hills. It was a simple shift dress, but maybe it was over the top here.

"Well, I like the ball cap version of you, but gorgeous superstar works, too."

"Thank you." She was way too pleased to find out that Joe liked the way she looked in a ball cap. What was wrong with her?

A knock at the back window interrupted the flirting. Goldie was grateful for that. She did not need to start something with this contractor and then break his heart when she left town.

"Hey, let me in!"

Libby and a tiny blonde woman were at the back porch door.

"What in the world, I thought we were meeting at seven?" Goldie ran over and let them in.

"Listen, you need to switch clothes with J.J."

"J.J.?"

"Yep, pretty good likeness, eh?"

J.J. had on a ton of makeup, eyelashes, and a blonde wig that looked like she was trying to do an impression of Goldie.

"What in the world?"

"Hey, Joe, do us a favor and look out the front to make sure no one's coming."

"Okay, yeah, sure."

Goldie had no idea what was happening. Libby grabbed Goldie's hands and started talking fast.

"Somehow, this TikTok kid spotted you at the hardware store. He's alerted the local fanboy contingent, and they're trying to find you. They're crawling all over town. They're asking where you lived, where you might be staying, if anyone's seen you at the grocery store."

"Ugh. Shoot. We were talking too loud, Joe, see?"

Joe shrugged.

"Look, switch with her."

With no regard to the fact that Joe was still in the vicinity,

Goldie took off her floral print dress and handed it to J.J., who ditched her cut-off shorts and Detroit Tigers t-shirt.

"Wow, J.J., whatever you're doing to stay fit is working. I'm the one they ask to do love scenes," Goldie said. She was impressed by how adorable J.J. was. Goldie spent half her waking hours working out and denying herself food.

"Thanks, I have a hula hoop. It works like a charm. Want a free peek there, Joe?"

"Nope, just on the lookout here. I don't need Dean rearranging my face, you evil temptresses."

"Hey, not too shabby," Libby remarked to J.J. "You two shorties are the same size, and with the wig, from far away, I'd be fooled."

"Thank you, let's hope they stay far away," J.J. said.

"Give her your hat."

J.J. plopped a Dean Construction trucker hat onto Goldie's head.

"Man, Dean's gonna want that on a poster someday," J.J. said.

"This is all well and good, switching, but I'm not clear on what's going on."

"J.J. is going out the front, all the way to the airport. We're gonna pretend you're flying out of here."

"Hope's out front with Aunt Emma's Lincoln Town Car. It's got tinted windows. Hope's your driver."

"Okay?"

"Except, you're not going to the airport. J.J. is."

J.J. struck a pose, back of her hand on her forehead. "No picture, no pictures!"

It was starting to get clearer.

"And where am I actually going?"

"On a boat ride," Libby said, grinning.

"In the words of Princess Leia, 'Here they come,'" Joe called to them from the window.

"I think you should haul out a few suitcases to really sell it," Libby said.

"Good idea." Goldie pointed to her room. She hadn't unpacked two of them, so it should be easy.

"Okay, so, if they're going to believe this, they can't get too close. What do you advise? You're the one with the Oscar."

Goldie looked at J.J. And assessed her best acting coach's advice.

"You're an open book, old friend, so maybe act like you're trying to hide. Like you know they're out there. But don't look straight at them. Also, don't be nice to Joe. Be the diva they think I am."

"Got it. Come on, beefcake. Let's hit it."

"Oh, and Hope is going to drive through town once," Libby explained. "At the stoplight, we'll roll the window down enough that they get a glimpse. They're congregating at Green and Lake Manitou."

"I'm going to be the best bait this lake has seen since Jared put filet minion on his hook after Mama brought it home in a doggie bag."

"Good luck," Libby said to J.J.

"You too."

Joe opened the door for J.J.

Goldie tried not to laugh, watching J.J. adopt a totally different posture. She was perfect. "Uh, maybe she is the real actress among us."

"She's for sure a ham," Libby replied.

"Now it's time for my performance?"

"You got it. We're going out the way I came in. And if anyone spots you, they'll think you're J.J.—they certainly won't think you're Goldie Hayes slumming it back here."

Goldie followed Libby out to the deck.

"The place doesn't have a working dock. I found that out a few days ago."

"Right, take off your tennis shoes."

Goldie did what Libby said. It was easy to fall right back into that dynamic. Libby was good at rallying the troops and, in this case, mounting a mobile diversionary operation.

"You're giving four-star general energy."

"Okay, then, march!"

They waded through the weeds and out to the water, right into the muck that Goldie had gotten stuck in on the first day. She still wasn't a fan, but with Libby's long legs and assured direction, Goldie didn't have a chance to really get grossed out.

The water was up to Goldie's knees and then, as they waded further out, her hips. She was falling behind.

Goldie tried to buck up and match her lanky friend, stride for stride, but wasn't succeeding.

Libby turned around and saw the struggle. "Here." Libby reached a hand back to Goldie.

"I can do it, I'm—whoa." She rethought her independence and grabbed Libby's hand.

"Okay, where's the little goldfish I grew up with?"

"It's ugh, well, I am used to poolside, I guess."

"You peeled a leech off your butt cheek with your bare hands without blinking an eye. Remember?"

Goldie remembered. Libby was right. She'd been so buffed, polished, and pampered lately that she'd forgotten how she used to be.

"Aha!" Libby waved her long arms, and a fancy-looking boat turned toward them.

"OOOH, that looks like something Jack Kennedy would take Jackie out on at *The Cape*." Goldie had played young Joan Kennedy in a miniseries back in the early aughts.

"Yeah, Keith's Chris-Craft is a beauty, isn't she?"

"Wow, okay, so is that George Clooney behind the wheel?"

"Do *not* tell Keith you think he looks like George Clooney."

"*That's* Keith? Wow, nice one, sister."

"Stop, but yeah, George Clooney wishes."

They held hands and started laughing. They were both more or less soaked.

"Stop, this is making me have to pee," Goldie said as the situation grew more and more absurd.

"Well, you're in the lake. Go for it."

"I mean, I am really falling down the shoot here now."

"There's not a potty on the boat, Goldie."

"Right."

A moment later, Keith got as close as he could get to them.

"You'll have to swim out. That seaweed is gonna muck up the engine. Hi, Goldie."

"Hey Keith, thanks for the lift."

"You okay to swim a few feet?"

"I am, I am."

Goldie took Libby's lead again, and they got close to the boat. Libby tread water easily, but Goldie wasn't as sure of herself.

"Here!" Keith flung a life preserver to Libby, and she slowly slid it over to Goldie.

"I'm really okay." As Goldie said it, a little lake water went up her nose.

"Take it. It will not be good for tourism if an Oscar winner drowns in Lake Manitou."

Goldie gratefully grabbed the life preserver. The little panic she had been starting to experience ebbed. They'd be fine. They'd be just fine.

"Get her first," Libby said as Keith put out a hand. Libby slid Goldie toward the boat.

"I got you." He grabbed her hand and lifted her ball cap to toes out of the water. She landed on the deck of the boat like a fish.

"Whoa, you're heavier than you look, bubble butt," Keith said and gave her a wink. He kneeled down and looked at her like he was a surgeon. He was the same old Keith, and she was inclined to either punch him in the shoulder or hug his neck.

"You're okay, just waterlogged." He was kind and patient with the antics of the Sandbar Sisters. In between teasing them. He really was an honorary member of the club.

"I'm okay."

"Okay, Q, get in here."

Libby was on the back of the boat. Goldie watched as her friend confidently used her arms to push herself up.

"Wow, someone has been doing her pushups," Goldie said.

"I've just been doing a lot of skiing. This one got tired of hauling me back in when I dumped."

"Never." Keith stood up and now reached over to Libby. He kissed her on the lips.

Goldie was amazed to see these two gorgeous adults together after all this time. She remembered the details of their breakup better than the plots of some of the movies she actually starred in.

"I've got some towels in the seat," Keith said.

Libby lifted the top of the bench seat and produced beach towels.

"You have my phone?" Libby asked Keith.

"Yeah. You want me to do a few slow circles?"

"I think it's best if we stay on the water until we know the diversion did the trick."

"Here, kiddo, dry off." Libby handed Goldie a towel and wrapped one around her own waist.

"Keith," Goldie said, "I can't believe we're all meeting here like this, again, after all this time."

Keith was behind the wheel of the boat now. He turned and smiled at Goldie. "We've always been so proud of you. I brag about you all the time. My sons do not believe I knew you when."

"How many?"

"Three boys. All smart as heck, their mom did a good job. Can't take any credit," Keith said.

Goldie noticed Libby smiling at the comment. "She sure did.

The world owes her a debt. The boys are great. Braylon works at Hope's place. He can make pastry that you'll die for."

"Margo had a heck of a sweet tooth."

From the conversation, it was clear to Goldie that Keith was a widower. Her heart broke a little for him. They all had stories. They all had full lives between the lake of 1989 and today.

The sun was warm. It helped make up for the fact that she was soaked.

"Ah ha!" Libby picked up her phone. "Victor, what's your vector?"

Goldie laughed. She wasn't sure when she'd laughed this much. Or when she'd last peed in a lake. Libby put her phone on speaker.

"Well, they bought it," J.J. said. "I had four cars trailing me. Hope is a speed demon. By the way, she is not authorized to drive the next time we road trip to Ann Arbor."

"You're exaggerating," Hope said.

"No, it's dramatic license. Look it up. Anyway, they followed all the way to the Lenawee County Airport. They helped us out of the car and unload bags at the airport. I made a real show of being in a panic. I am telling you, doing hair was the wrong career choice."

"They followed all the way, took pictures, from the fence. They thought it was Goldie," Hope said.

"Okay, so we need to be sure. You're heading to town?"

"Yep, we're checking the hashtag online. It looks like the pictures are showing up. The fanboys are trying to figure out where Goldie's headed. But they're sure she's not here. They're all theorizing. I think it worked."

"Great."

"I'm swinging by to pick up the dinner from the restaurant, and do you want to change?"

"Heck no, I'm going to dress like this for Dean. It'll spice things up."

"TMI," Hope said. "We'll do a circle around town, make sure no one is snooping there too. But things are looking pretty quiet, situation ghost town once again."

"Okay. So, rendezvous at Nora House, ninety minutes or so? And make sure Joe knows he's invited. He was critical to Operation Get Goldie Gone."

Libby ended the call.

Goldie leaned back in her seat on the boat. She looked at Keith and Libby. They had gone to the end of the earth to protect her just now. While Hollis had sold her out for money, her old friends had done the opposite.

She also realized that not only had they diverted the press. They had done so to the detriment of their main goal, to get people to Irish Hills.

"Irish Hills was crawling with people, for a hot second. That was weird," Keith commented, as though reading her thoughts.

"Yeah, there was almost a traffic jam," Libby said.

"You could have capitalized on this," Goldie said. "You could have called more press in. That would change the game for tourism. I'm more famous than Chef Ellston, if I do say so."

"Damn straight you are, but you're our friend. Not our meal ticket."

"But, I mean, I just—"

"—I promised you that you would be safe here, that you could rest here. I was serious about that."

Goldie wanted to thank them. She wanted them to know how much of a revelation this was to her. Everyone in her life lived off of her or tried to sell a piece of her.

Keeping her secret was in direct opposition to what all of her old friends were trying to do. But they'd done it anyway.

Half a dozen people that she hadn't seen in more than two dozen years had gone bananas to keep her hidden.

Goldie let that fact sink in. And she started to wonder, what could she do to show how much it meant to her?

Chapter Sixteen

Goldie

They enjoyed dinner at Nora House, Goldie in a borrowed sweatshirt from Libby and J.J. in the dress Goldie had lent her.

It was a mishmash of her old friends and her new handyman, and it was the most fun she'd had since she didn't know when.

They talked about the old days, and Joe listened intently.

"I mean, this is the one you said peeled the leech off her backside without flinching?"

"She didn't bat an eye. The raft, unbeknownst to us, had a little pocket of them. They decided to take up residence under the raft and wait. We're laying there, baking ourselves like lasagna, a little red crispiness was the goal, and Goldie turned over, ya gotta have an even tan, you know, and there the sucker was. Right on her cheek," J.J. recounted the scene to Joe.

"Literally," Hope said.

"That was no big deal. The big deal was later that summer. I got knocked off the Hobie, clocked right in the head by the boom, and went into the water."

"Oh, that was scary, not funny," Keith said.

"She was out cold, and Libby here dives in immediately, swims to her, puts her in the official lifeguard hold, and swims back to shore, Goldie in tow."

Joe looked from Keith to Libby.

"Yeah, the boat was tipped at that point," Libby explained.

"No life jackets back then, very dumb kids, obviously."

"Yeah, it was the eighties, no helmets or life jackets, very dumb," Goldie said. She reached out and squeezed Libby's hand. A teenage Goldie had been unconscious in the water, and her friend had saved her.

Why had she never unpacked these memories? She had so many here, in Irish Hills. But it seemed like, from the moment she left, she used every cell of her brain toward becoming a star. She didn't have room to think about nostalgia or the gang at the lake.

"We drank pop and ate pop rocks at the same time. It was madness," Hope said.

They reminisced, ate, drank, and watched the sun go down over Lake Manitou.

It was late July. Something about that time of year here let you know that things were fleeting. That summer was exiting faster than it entered. And you better squeeze every drop of sunlight out of the days. Maybe it was a Michigan thing. In California, July didn't produce fear that the sunny days were on the way out. Maybe in Michigan, scarcity made you better appreciate days like today.

"So, what's on the menu this week," Libby asked Hope.

"Ah, about that, I don't think we can open until Saturday."

"Why?"

"The server issue, I'm down to two right now. We're just not getting the customers to sustain them. Tips are their livelihood, you know?"

"Shoot, if I could just figure out how to pump up the eyeballs."

"Isn't North of Nash next week? My son's a big fan. That ought to be a boon," Joe said.

"What's North of Nash?" Goldie asked.

"For the past few years, there's this gigantic country music festival at the racetrack. I mean massive," J.J. explained.

"If a tiny fraction, a tiny fraction of a fraction of that crowd came over to Irish Hills, that would make a nice impact. Which might work for next year, but this year I didn't have lodging to offer or even a restaurant until a few weeks ago. So, well, I couldn't really lure anyone."

"You've done so much, so fast. We'll survive the summer and plan for next, when we blow it out of the water," J.J. said.

But Hope looked more sheepish and less confident. If she didn't have a staff, she didn't have a restaurant. Judging by the food that Hope had served tonight, the restaurant was probably amazing.

"Ugh, we shouldn't have hid me. I should have put a flag hat on and said come and get me, I'll be at the Green Street stop light." Goldie wanted to help, but she didn't want to be the subject of any more flying water bottles.

"We know your Hollywood people sold you out. Irish Hills will not get it," J.J. said.

"Exactly," Libby said.

J.J. squeezed Goldie's shoulder.

But Goldie could see the worry in all their eyes. They had a mission to save Irish Hills. It was important to them. But they hadn't given her up to accomplish it.

Goldie would figure out something to pay them back.

* * *

The next day she checked to make sure her little publicity stunt had worked.

"Well, you've created a mystery. Nice job."

133

Hedda had called her this time. There were no script offers or event requests in her inbox. But the press inquiries were tenfold, according to Tally.

Goldie was in demand. At least, an interview with her was a hot ticket. No one was brave enough to cast her while she was on the outs with the Victor Superhero Universe machine. But she'd scored a little victory of her own.

"Thank you. Now, about managing the next phase of my career. I'm willing to listen to your pitch."

"I don't have the pitch for you yet. I think your current strategy of staying under wraps is still a good one. And you're currently not on my roster. Don't forget, I need the boys who run the VSU happy, too. It's their town right now."

Goldie ignored the fact that Hedda hadn't agreed to represent her. She was still somewhat shocked to be in this position at this stage of her career. But nevertheless, Hedda was giving her advice, inching closer with each phone call to making it official.

"I've got some very quiet meetings going on here. It's time I took control of my projects. Like Reece does, if you want to be on board with that kind of vision. I'd consider it."

"Ha, interesting. I do have some good news. Your old friend Tommy, the DP on that picture, let me know that what they saw of Trevor's footage, it was shaping up to be a cacophonous mess."

"That tracks, shooting it was a cacophonous mess."

"I haven't seen anything with you in it, so that's good news. No matter what Trevor says about you, it would be quite a trick to mess up the scenes you weren't even in."

"Thanks, yeah, faint praise there."

"Well, if I'm going to represent you, we need to build on what we can."

"So, you're in?"

"Yes, tentatively. Now go get the next the rights to the next *Gone Girl* book or whatever you're after. That would be big."

"I need a favor. Can you tell me who represents Chase Green, uh, Luke Brush, and River Ann Flowers?"

"What? Yeah, they're with DAA."

"Great, I had a little idea for them. Appreciate it."

Goldie thought there was something she could do when it came to the country music scene and Irish Hills. She roped Tally into her plan. Fairly easily, the two of them had emails and DMs for most of the artists at North of Nash.

There was more than one way to get people talking about Irish Hills.

Goldie
2018

"I thought you were coming with me? I'd really like it if you could make the drive with me."

Goldie was scared. She didn't scare easily, but she was scared this time.

"Here's the thing. You want privacy. You don't want people to know about this. If I go, you know how that will be."

Goldie wanted coffee. She couldn't have coffee. She wasn't supposed to have anything before the surgery. The lack of caffeine was making the headache of trying to understand Drake's reasoning even more difficult than usual.

She and Drake had been together for three years. They more or less lived together, but they both had their own places. They had an escape hatch, as it were, in case. In case what? The sad fact was they had an escape hatch in case they didn't work out.

Drake was the lead singer of Burgundy Four. The country music group was going on five years of hits, one after the other. Their biggest hit, 'Summer Smile,' was famously about Goldie.

Drake had worked for years to hit big. He'd been the lead

singer of three bands that never went anywhere, and then finally with Burgundy Four, and a country twist, then boom.

The magic and the work he'd put in combined at the right time. He was the hottest thing going in today's country music. He spoke with a drawl, and no one seemed to ask him about actually being from New Jersey.

That gap of time, though, meant Drake was in his forties when he hit big. They were the same age, but he was playing it younger. Way younger. Of course, he was a man, so he looked like he was in his twenties. And any mention of his age listed him in his early thirties. He was hanging on to that youth fan base as hard as he could, as tightly as he could.

Goldie was headed to the hospital for a hysterectomy. Not the chicest of surgical procedures. Everyone on her team told her to keep it quiet. Fibroids were not the disease of the week. Girlfriend in the hospital for fibroids was not a sexy story to sell to Drake's fan base, apparently.

"You'll be fine. This is a run-of-the-mill thing. They do it all the time."

Goldie looked at Drake, really looked at him.

Drake was ripped. He was all sinew and muscle.

To the outside world, it appeared that Drake Denver was into hard partying. He was country music's bad boy. He had more tattoos than she could count. He acted like Jack Daniels was in his cup on stage, but the reality was that he worked hard to look underfed. He was drinking bone broth and getting HCG injections, not heroin. All to stay young for the fans.

She could relate.

She was Drake's dream woman; he'd said it over and over again. He'd written about it in his music. He'd swept her off her feet. When he got famous, he'd made a beeline to Goldie Hayes. And it worked. She was enamored.

He was funny, too. They laughed when they were together. And he seemed to need her in a way her other relationships hadn't.

He wanted her to listen to his music, his lyrics, and even weigh in on things like his onstage performances. He was protective of her when they were surrounded by paparazzi.

And she knew that being with him made her seem younger, cooler, hipper than she was.

When they weren't in the public eye, they both liked reading, listening to music, and even watching Netflix. It all worked. They weren't living together or married, but still, it felt real as anything else Goldie had been involved in.

And she needed him now, as she faced her surgery. She was scared. If he would just be there at the hospital to talk with her beforehand, that would be so nice. Shouldn't he want to if he cared about her?

"Still, it's not run of the mill to me."

"I hate hospitals, you know that. It reminds me of death and my dad and all that."

Drake's family life was a wreck. She did know that.

And he was right. There would be a higher chance of the press finding out about her hysterectomy if Drake was there.

"Okay, yeah, you're right. Just be there after? Maybe when I wake up?"

"Ah, yes, okay. I'll have them smuggle me in."

"Also, smuggle in coffee. I'm going to be going on two days without it. I think my head might explode."

It was early. Goldie wanted to go in before anyone was awake. That, too, would help her keep her secret. Drake went back to sleep. It was Hollis who drove Goldie to the hospital.

She checked in alone. She was in surgery prep alone. And she felt like she might be having a panic attack before the surgery, alone.

The anesthesiologist came in to talk to her beforehand.

The doctor was young and cool and looked like she could be in Burgundy Four, too. She had nearly as many tats as Drake.

"I just want to check in. You're okay?"

"I'm freaking the heck out."

"You know what, we can up your medication a bit. That nervousness will go away in a second."

"Yes, please. Also, coffee, I am going to wake up from this needed caffeine. Like really need it. I'm addicted."

"I'll put it in your chart, no worries, it'll be bedside, or I'll zing a little caffeine in your I.V." The doctor winked.

It helped. She was so nice. "My boyfriend is going to be in the recovery room, so he knows, too."

"Sounds like a plan. We gotchu, Ms. Hayes."

"Thanks, call me Goldie."

The meds were kicking in. Her worries were evaporating, along with the ability to keep her eyes open.

She remembered being wheeled down a hall. She remembered saying hello to her doctor. And that was it. That was all.

Hours later, she was still in the bed, alone. She was struggling to open her eyes.

Her head hurt. Was she in for brain surgery?

There was no one to ask. Nurses bustled around, but no one stopped.

She closed her eyes again, but the pain in her head was getting stronger.

"Can someone...?"

Goldie felt like she was in a dream. Inside she was screaming, but all she could manage was a week croaking sound.

Finally, a nurse approached the bed. "Ms. Hayes, hello. You're coming out of it. Wonderful."

"I need caffeine."

"Yes, here, let me pour you a cup of coffee."

She drank a sip. It dribbled down the front of her gown. She tried again. This time with a modicum of success.

"Where's Drake? Can he come in now?"

"Uh, who?"

"My boyfriend."

The nurse left to check.

Goldie took another sip of coffee. She wanted to sit up. Could she sit up?

The nurse returned.

"There's no one in the waiting room. But if you like, I can call someone for you."

"No, no, it's okay. Can I sit up?"

"Give it a little time, maybe in about half an hour. The doctor will swing by in a bit."

"Uh, nurse, am I okay?"

"You're fine, flying colors."

"Thank you."

The nurse left to attend to other patients. Slowly, Goldie got less groggy. The doctor talked to her. She could leave today. As planned.

Drake never showed.

She'd thought he would drive her home.

A nurse helped her get dressed. Put her in the wheelchair. She called Scott Ozock. Of course, he didn't answer. His assistant did, and the assistant called for a car for her.

If Mitchell was still alive, he'd have come. Her mom was too old now to travel cross country, and her dad had been gone for over a decade. She was sitting in a wheelchair in the lobby, alone. She had a hat and sunglasses on. No one would recognize her, just like Scott Ozock advised.

"Don't be seen. Don't tell anyone you have fibroids. That's not sexy."

No, it was not sexy in the least bit.

She'd done everything they'd told her to get where she was. She'd sacrificed a lot to be here. But right now, here, she was alone, with five incisions from a robot arm and a stranger taking her home to her mansion in the hills.

Where was Drake?

Eventually, she was home, in her own bed. She had pain meds.

That was something.

Drake showed up the next day. She needed a shower. But she was afraid to stand by herself.

"Can you help me?"

Drake looked at her with an expression she didn't understand at first. And then it dawned on her. He was disgusted. Or maybe it was fear.

"Forget it. Can you just leave?"

"Don't be dramatic."

"I needed you, and you weren't there. Just leave."

"Medical stuff, you know I can't—"

"—Whatever."

"I'm sorry, I know I should have, but I think we need to end this."

"I think so, too. Just make sure you take all your stuff. I don't want the clutter."

"I owe you so much. You really helped me navigate the—"

"—Let's not, okay? Goodbye."

You can't make a person into someone else. Drake wanted her to take care of him, and he had no capacity to give that back to her. He did owe her so much. But she didn't even have the energy to collect.

And she reminded him that he was old. Maybe that was her worst quality.

Eventually, she took a shower. Eventually, her current assistant arrived and helped her hire a nurse.

But for six weeks, she hid.

Her only comfort was from calls with Siena. Siena and her mom called, sent flowers, sent candy, and Face Timed her. They were there, even though they weren't. Goldie assured them that it was okay, that the surgery was no big deal.

In a lot of ways, she was right. It was no big deal. Goldie healed fast. She felt pretty good after two weeks and just about normal after two months.

But the idea that she'd gone through it alone was in the back of her mind. She'd sacrificed a lot for this life.

And it was coming home to roost.

Chapter Seventeen

Goldie, Present Day

Goldie spent the morning on the computer. She'd sent invites and personal notes. Left messages on private lines and slid in the DMs of a few of the country music stars on the schedule for North of Nash. All but one. She wanted to help Irish Hills, but she had her limits.

By then, she was pleased with herself. If she couldn't be the draw for Irish Hills, maybe she could lean on a few other big names to add some sparkle in the form of rhinestones to the local scene.

She didn't tell a soul about what she was doing. She just reached out with invitations.

Up next on her list of things to do, was a meeting with Joe Cassidy about working for her instead of Libby.

Joe arrived early. He was always early. This was opposite of a Hollywood power play.

Goldie was out on the back lawn, looking at the mess that was the reedy overgrowth.

"This feels like an issue. Back in the day, guests could hang out back here, there was the dock and a huge slide, and there was a shuffleboard area somewhere around here. Right now, it's not great for swimming."

"Hi, Joe, how are you?"

"Well, you are ten minutes early, always on Lombardi Time."

"Whoa, you know what that is?"

"My dad swore by it. If you're on time, you're late."

"Exactly, good man."

"Anyway, I was going to head in to talk to you. But this vegetation situation distracted me. I need to hire someone."

"My son could do it. If you want. Red charges reasonable rates."

"Oh, yes, can you ask him? Also, that leads me to the next item on my list. What about you? How long do I have you?"

Joe gave her a wicked look, and Goldie actually felt herself blush. She, the woman used to ignoring depraved producers flashing her from under their hotel robes, she actually blushed.

"I have blocked out the rest of the summer, maybe into fall, for this job. That was Libby's deal anyway, same for you?"

"Do you think everything will be done by then?"

"Done? This place will never be done. You have a thirteen-bedroom monster on the lake. It will always need to be cared for, probably full time."

"Is that something you do?"

"I do historic restoration. That's my line. But Libby and Dean knew I was between jobs, so they locked me in for the time being. And I do love this old place."

"I need you." Goldie said it wrong. "I mean, I need you to help get this place in shape."

Goldie's weird declaration did not go unnoticed by Joe. He smirked at her, and she had the urge to punch him in the chest. But that wouldn't be professional. She was already the diva from Hollywood.

"I can't stay here forever, but I can get you on your feet. Until my next job comes around."

"Great, Libby told me your rate. I'm going to double it."

"What, you're nuts!"

"No, I just want to hedge a little against that next job."

Take that, Mr. Flirt, she thought. Goldie was not strapped for cash. She might be a fish out of water in the water. She might not be the same girl who didn't flinch at a leech on her backside, but she wasn't without resources. Financial and otherwise.

"I'll give you until the end of the season."

"Great. I'm probably going to have to leave before then, and I'll want to know that we're well at hand with repairs."

"So, back to Hollywood?"

"I have a major career to tend to. Yes, back to Hollywood, but for now, let 'em miss me."

"Got it. So, today's agenda, that raccoon trap."

"We're setting it up?"

"Ha, no, we're letting little Ricky the Raccoon out. He's up there. Didn't you hear the squeaking?"

"No, I sleep with noise-canceling headphones."

"Well, it's attic time for me, you game?"

"I mean, yeah?"

Goldie was game. If nothing else, all this could serve as research if she ever booked a horror movie. Creeping around an old attic, she'd know exactly what emotions to summon.

Joe and Goldie traveled up the stairs to the massive attic.

"There it is. The trap did its job."

"Is she okay?"

"Yes, but we're going to need to restore this attic. It's a mess."

"Yeah, it is."

Goldie didn't like the look of things up here. Not that she knew what it was supposed to look like, but she had envisioned vintage furniture or dusty Victrolas. Not shredded insulation and raccoon droppings. She put her hand over her nose. She also started to rethink her impulse to buy this place.

"Don't move. It's probably not safe. I can't see where I want you to walk."

"Not safe?"

"Hang on. I'm calling my guy."

Goldie didn't want to get too close to the raccoon trap. And the raccoon seemed okay with that as well. She did as Joe said, and he finished his call.

Goldie stepped around the chewed-up insulation. She started to feel sort of ill.

"Ah, I'm going to get out of here."

"Watch where you step."

"I need to get out of here." She was sick to her stomach.

The smell and the heat were maybe too much. She did not want to faint or vomit in front of Joe. She ignored his advice to step carefully in an effort to stave off the scene she was sure was about to go down.

"This attic floor has some weak spots. You don't want to—"

She felt a wave of nausea and lunged for the attic door. She ran down the steps as fast as possible. That was it. She was going to hurl. Nothing was more important than getting to a bathroom at that moment.

She ran to the first one on the third-floor hall and ralphed, as J.J. called it back in the day, into the sink. Lucky, it was mostly liquid. Coffee was the only thing in her stomach so far today.

She turned on the faucet and splashed water on her face. She took a few breaths. She was feeling better already.

She heard heavy footsteps behind her.

"Give me a minute."

"Are you okay?"

"A minute."

"I'm not going anywhere."

She looked at herself in the pocked mirror. Offhandedly,

Goldie wondered about each bathroom. Did they all need new mirrors?

She was pale, had a little chill as her body adjusted to leaving the attic heat, and she felt a little burning sensation on her legs.

Whatever, she was fine. She leaned down and drank a little water from the tap. She swished it around her mouth. Joe knocked on the door again.

"I'm coming in if you don't come out."

"It's fine. I'm fine." Goldie turned off the water and walked out to find Joe, looking more concerned than the situation required.

"If something is wrong, you don't run away from help."

"Ah, you're bossing me now?"

"You could have fallen down those steps or through the insulation. I said stay still."

"I got sick to my stomach, not a biggie. It's not exactly fresh up there, and you know, it's hot."

"Still." Joe appeared to be looking her up and down.

Goldie reached down and rubbed her ankles. They felt irritated.

"What's wrong?"

"My legs, uh, sting a little."

"Okay, you need to take a shower. A cold shower. Do not rub your ankles. Try not to itch them either. I think fiberglass particles are on your ankles. That's what's stinging. It's from the old insulation. When you shower, you want the pores to stay closed. Understand? And do you have aloe vera?"

"I do."

"Use that after you take your cold shower. It'll calm the skin. We've got to remove the insulation up there. We're going to have to do foam. You're too sensitive to fiberglass. I shouldn't have let you up there."

"Let me? I own the place."

"You're not going up again. It's my job anyway."

"And don't you have a raccoon in a cage to manage? I'll deal with my own issues."

"Crap, yes, I do. Okay. Rinse off, I'll get rid of the critter, and you stay out of the attic."

"Sounds like a plan." Goldie did think a shower was in order after her attic experience.

"I'm going to have my buddy pick up the raccoon. I'll be on the grounds, but text me if you're nauseous again. Or if you need anything."

"Thanks."

"Don't put those clothes in your normal hamper."

"What?"

"Just put them on the floor. I'll come to get them in a garbage bag. They're not expensive, I hope."

Goldie did not have a gauge for what Joe thought was expensive.

Goldie did as Dr. Joe instructed.

Her phone buzzed with a text every ten minutes. Each time, it was Joe.

You okay?

Remember not to itch.

Go easy on the aloe vera. You don't want to rub it in hard.

At first, it was annoying, and then, it started to dawn on her what was happening. Joe gave a darn. He was legitimately worried about her.

After she was showered, changed, and feeling a million times better, she went outside to find him. Joe was waving to a man driving a truck that was leaving the property.

"Ricky the Raccoon taking a trip?"

"It's all humane. He'll take him to the woods, where he can't eat insulation or poo inside."

"Good, that makes me happy. So, what's next on the agenda for the day?"

"I would think you firing me."

"What?"

"I shouldn't have let you in the attic. I should have checked your footwear. That's inexcusable."

"Please, it's fine. I'm not going to fire you."

"I think you might because things are about to get awkward."

Before she could ask him what he meant, Joe swept her up in his arms and kissed her. It wasn't shy or tentative. He was sweaty and tasted salty. She kissed him right back.

And then he let her go and looked her straight in the eye. "See...things could get awkward."

"I like awkward. Now get back to work. This hotel won't renovate itself."

Goldie turned around. She had no plan on where she was headed, but she knew she needed to have a cute exit.

She walked through the kitchen, out the side door, and out into the grounds.

She'd been in dozens of romantic movies, in several real-life passionate love affairs, but Joe Cassidy, contractor, in a tenth of a second, had blown away some of the most famous heartthrobs on the planet in the kissing department.

"Well, all be darned." She looked back at the hotel.

Where was she going to say she went after she walked away from his kiss?

She hadn't thought that far ahead as she made her adorable exit. For the first time since she didn't know when, she was flustered by a man.

Since the utter disappointment of her relationship with Drake, she hadn't been interested in anyone. Nor did she "put herself out there" for dating. Besides, most people used apps these days, and she barely knew how to update her phone.

Wow, though. That was some kiss.

She looked down at her phone.

That's it. That's what she could do to act like kissing Joe Cassidy wasn't the only thing on her mind all of a sudden. She'd call someone and act like she had Hollywood business to take care of.

After all, soon she should start hearing from all the country stars she'd invited to Irish Hills.

She'd spent the morning reaching out. They were literally just up the road. She'd invited them all to come to have the best meal of their lives at Hope's Plate.

She was an A-list actress, and people responded to her texts. They answered her calls.

There was a smattering of responses. But all from personal assistants. Could Goldie Hayes not even get a return message these days?

Was this fallout from the VSU thing?

Or were they just too busy?

That was possible. Goldie was going to have to go further out on a limb to help Irish Hills.

She walked back into Two Lakes.

She did not want to do this, but she was going to.

"Joe?"

"Yeah, in here."

She walked into the tight space that was the ancient laundry room. Joe was handsome. That was just a fact. It distracted her for a beat.

"You come back here to slap me retroactively?"

She shook her head. "No, two things. One, I need a ride to North of Nash. I'm going to help Irish Hills my way, and that means I'm going to have to call in a favor."

"Okay, sure, we can go there. The traffic's a bear, but I know a guy who might be able to get us through a back way."

"Great."

"And the second thing?"

Goldie took a step toward Joe. Pulled him down to her level by his neck. She kissed him. He smelled good. Not like cologne, just good.

She stepped back, and they locked eyes.

"Wow."

"Now, I'm going to get changed. I have to look like Goldie Hayes for this next bit."

"Who do you look like now?"

"Elizabeth Gould."

"Ah, I see. Well, I'll get the truck ready and call my friend."

* * *

They drove back roads, some she recognized and remembered. Others she didn't. If Goldie thought she was staying here more permanently, she'd have to get a driver's license again. But for now, it was a novelty for her to ride in the passenger seat instead of the back, with a screen between her and her driver.

"There's Greg."

A man was standing next to an SUV. He didn't have a uniform on, but he looked official. Joe slowed down and opened his window.

"Hey Greg, thank you for doing this. She walks through the main entrance, and there's sure to be a scene."

"No problem, a friend of Hope's is a friend of mine."

Goldie had heard Hope was a little more than neighborly with her neighbor. This must be him.

"You're Hope's neighbor?"

"That I am, and a big fan of your movies. Honored to help." He nodded as he said it.

The men around here could be so old-fashioned. It was charming and unexpected.

"Just follow me. I'll get you backstage. There's a drop-off area and a service truck area. I think with this, you're best in the service truck area."

"Lead the way."

Joe followed Greg past a drive with a sign marking the main

entrance. Instead, they entered a different drive with a gate. There was also a man checking I.D. Greg said something to him, and then the security guard looked back toward Joe and Goldie. He waved them through.

"Okay, looks like we're all clear," Joe said.

Goldie tried to get a good look at the setup for North of Nash. It was a mass of people on the infield of the track, rocking out to the act on the main stage. The stage had a long runway, so the performers could walk out amongst the crowds but not be swallowed by them. Which looked like a real possibility.

The track was surrounded by stadium-style seating, but no one was in those seats. They were all on that infield. In the distance, Goldie spied hundreds of campers and RVs.

"It's NASCAR here, right, normally?"

"That it is, ma'am. You a fan?"

"I was up for the role of a young Martha Earnhardt, Dale's mother, a while back. Did my research."

"Oh?"

"Yeah, didn't get it. They went with Frances McDormand."

North of Nash was an enormous event. That much was clear. Throngs were crowded around the stage where Luke Brush was performing, currently.

"Wow, it's nuts."

"Yeah, it's like a country music Woodstock but every year. Last year they clocked forty thousand attendees."

The crowd scared Goldie a little. It was massive. She was happy when Joe's truck was fully obscured by the backstage area. This was just as chaotic, but it wasn't the press of humanity on the other side of the stage.

"Well, I don't think Irish Hills can handle an influx of four thousand, much less forty, but if my plan works, we'll get some buzz going."

"Okay, so edify me here. We were disguising you before, making sure everyone didn't know you were in town. And now, well, you look like a movie star, and we are very squarely in Lenawee County, Michigan. Anyone sees you, aren't you in the same boat as the other day?"

"Here's the thing, I'm not a country star. These fans are going to be looking for Dolly, not Goldie. Those fanboys were stalking me specifically. Here, hopefully, no one's looking. And I have to look like I belong backstage, right? I mean, security has to believe I'm Goldie Hayes. Do I look like Goldie Hayes?"

"Spitting image."

Joe parked in a section where his truck looked like half a dozen others. There were food trucks, electrical equipment trucks, satellite trucks, and others. There were dozens of service vehicles needed to put on this kind of event without a hitch.

There were also tents and trailers for the performers. Goldie was zoning in on a specific tour bus. She'd never traveled in it. But she did know it when she saw it.

"I think you're going to want to hang here by your truck."

"I agree, not keen on letting you wander off, but if someone realizes I don't have credentials, I think they'll tow me."

"Back in a flash. I hope."

Goldie left Joe and headed for the deep red tour bus. She'd help select the logo. It looked great emblazoned on the side of the enormous bus. Sometimes the band traveled in it, sometimes it was a diversion, but for this event, she hoped they'd be in there. At least while they waited until their time on stage. She'd checked the schedule. They were performing on the main stage tonight and then again, midday Sunday.

She fixed her best movie star haughty, entitled, let me in without checking, attitude.

She knocked on the Burgundy Four tour bus door. Drake's tour manager answered. She'd met him multiple times, but it took a second for him to register who she was. Casey Long's job was to get Drake where he was supposed to be, on time, and to be sure whatever Drake needed was at the venue. Whether it was food or female companionship. She never caught Drake cheating when they were together, but then again, she never tried to.

"I, uh, Ms. Hayes, what are you, uh." He looked confused, and for a second, panicked.

"I'm in the neighborhood, here to see Drake."

Goldie put her hand out for him to help her up the high steps. He did, as she expected, without thinking.

"GREAT TO SEE YOU, GOLDIE," Casey Long said, announcing her presence as loud as he could.

Goldie was one hundred percent clear on what Casey was doing. His boss, Drake, was likely canoodling with someone. Something that Goldie did not care one lick about. But that was another one of the jobs the tour manager had on his plate. He was charged with making sure the boss didn't get caught with his leather pants down.

She smiled as Casey walked toward the back of the bus and knocked loudly.

"Drake, hate to disturb your Zoom call, but you have a visitor."

"Zoom call?" Goldie tried not to roll her eyes but failed.

He knocked again, and midway through, Drake opened the door.

"What the?" He was shirtless, and his pants were on, but barely.

"I see you've got some fresh ink there, Drake."

"Goldie." He moved forward and appeared genuinely happy to see her, and then looked back, realizing that his Zoom call had come to life and followed him out of the bedroom.

The Zoom call was a beautiful young thing. Goldie thought she recognized her from somewhere.

"Hello, I'm Goldie Hayes," she said to the young lady.

"No way, no WAY!"

"Way. Listen, I'm so sorry to just drop in, but I'm taking a little break here in Michigan. And saw you were on the North of Nash schedule, and well, I wanted to invite you to a get-together just up the road. You and the band, and—"

Though the woman was familiar, Goldie couldn't quite place her name.

"River Ann Flowers," she offered brightly.

"Yes, I voted for you on *The Voice*!" She hadn't, but she'd seen the show, and it snapped back into place, just in time.

"I'm dying, no way. No WAY!"

"Way. Drake, I know it's sort of short notice, but this would be my treat. I'd love to host you at this great local restaurant. I guarantee it'll be the best meal you're ever going to have, trust me. Plus, you could be away from the melee for a bit."

"Thanks, but I don't think—"

He was totally off balance. They hadn't seen each other in years, and here she was on his tour bus in Michigan.

"Chef Venerable is amazing. She's like the next big thing. You'd be able to charge your batteries."

"She won The World's Best Dishes Food Competition!"

"You're a foodie?" Goldie directed her attention to River Ann.

"I love the food shows and the competitions. If I could cook, I'd have entered that instead of The Voice." She laughed at her own joke, and Goldie did, too. The girl was charming, and her energy was infectious. She seemed about a decade and a half too young for Drake, but he was immature, so maybe it was perfect.

"Her new place is all local, incredible peak of the season dining."

"We have to do it, Drake, we have to!"

Goldie had an ally she hadn't expected. "Like I said, it's on me," she assured them. "I promise it will be the meal of your lives."

River Ann clapped her hands in approval.

"Can you give us a minute, babe?" Drake said to River Ann.

"Yep, sure, can I invite my backup singers? Would that be too much?"

"I haven't even said we're doing this."

Goldie looked at River Ann and nodded yes, with a wink.

"He'll do it. He does whatever I say." River Ann returned the wink and made her way to the door of the tour bus.

"I'll make sure he gives me your digits," Goldie told her. "I'll text you."

River Ann bounded out of the bus. She took the youth that Drake was hanging on to with her.

"Well, she seems a bit to keep up with. Congrats."

"Yeah, I guess it's a good problem."

"I'd say."

Drake found a shirt and squirmed into it. He was still lean as ever.

"I liked you in *Dusty Trail*. I always thought you had it in you to be a good actor." Goldie wasn't blowing smoke. Drake had a featured role in the limited series, and he was good. Surprisingly so.

"Thanks, well, Tim McGraw sets that standard, but I didn't do too badly."

"You did great, so how about it? Come out to dinner?"

"Why do you want us to? Why now?"

"I need to borrow your heat."

"What?"

"I'm getting dogged lately by fans of VSU, they're hating me, long story, but I want to help bump tourism in this little town, Irish Hills, where the restaurant is, but I can't do it myself."

"Why?"

"I'm supposed to be in hiding. I'm trying not to attract attention."

"That dress is the opposite of that, just so you know." He gave her a look that used to work like a charm.

It didn't anymore, hmm. That knowledge was worth the little trip here, even if he didn't accept her invite to Irish Hills.

"Ha, thanks. What do you say? Help me out? I mean, when we broke up, you told me you owed me, remember? I mean, the logo on the bus is an example."

She'd helped a lot back when Drake and Burgundy Four were exploding in popularity. She knew the ropes of fame and helped him navigate some of the early pitfalls. And yet he couldn't be bothered to come to the hospital when she asked.

"Yeah. I was an idiot. That was crummy of me not to come, when, you know. Just disappearing."

"Kind of, but I survived. And you're with River Ann, so it all worked out."

It had all worked out, but Goldie had been depressed and disappointed back then. Drake had seemed like the last love of her life. The idea that he wasn't was only now starting to blossom. She'd gotten over it, but it had taken time.

"So, what's the deal, we come out to Hope's, whatever it's called in Irish something or other, and you buy us dinner?"

"Yes. And have your people do some social on it."

"Alright, I actually don't think I have a choice. River Ann gets her way in all things."

Goldie felt a tad sorry for Drake all of a sudden. He seemed to be every decade of his almost fifty years in relation to keeping up with a twenty-something.

"Great, and if you could look, ugh, well, every inch Burgundy Four, that would be great."

"So, not completely off the clock, eh?"

"Drake, you know I wouldn't ask if it wasn't important."

"I know. Good to see you."

"Good to see you, and I'll see you tomorrow night. I promise it is way better than a hospital bedside."

"Oh ouch."

"Same cell?"

"Yeah."

"I'll text you and Casey the details."

"Fine, fine, but you know River Ann is gluten-free," Drake said.

"Got it."

Goldie had what she needed, a promise from Drake, his band, and the bonus of River Ann. As she headed back to Joe and the truck. On her way, she ran into River Ann again.

"Thanks so much for your help with Drake. You guys will have a great time. I promise, and you know, totally bring your backup singers and anyone else who's around tomorrow night who needs a nice dinner away from the melee."

"Really?"

"Really."

River Ann squealed like she'd won the speed round on *Family Feud*. Goldie laughed and left her new friend to invite whoever she wanted.

She caught back up with Joe, who was surrounded by a few lovely country music groupies.

She listened as he explained that no, he wasn't Tim McGraw.

"Just a carpenter. I promise. And he's way shorter than me, I'm pretty sure."

"Come on, Tim, we need to get rolling. Sorry, ladies."

"We *knew* it was you."

Joe looked at her like she was insane. "You're not helping," Joe said.

Goldie kept a straight face.

"Can we get an autograph or a selfie or—"

"—Listen, we're running late, but if you want to catch a glimpse of him tomorrow, he likes to shop in this little place called Irish Hills, just up the road."

The girls seemed positively berserk over that.

"You're a lot shorter than I thought," one of the girls said. This time it was Goldie's height in question.

"Yeah, I'm taking a selfie to prove we met you two."

Before Goldie could protest, the girls had their backs to her, their cameras in the air, and were snapping pics.

"Wow, Tim McGraw and Faith Hill, we're hitting the jackpot!"

Goldie got in the truck. If they posted to social, none of the fanboys would care. She looked nothing like Faith Hill. These poor kids were likely drunk or needed their eyes checked.

"We better get out of her before they realize we're neither of those two."

Joe slowly navigated his truck through the maze that was the VIP backstage area, and once they got back on M-50, Joe asked the question.

"Okay, so what was that all about? I think you owe good ole Tim McGraw the details."

Goldie was pleased with herself, and now that it looked like she'd succeeded, she spilled her guts.

"I've got about half a dozen country music stars headed to Irish Hills."

"Yeah, when?"

"Tomorrow. Can you take me to Nora House? I need to fill Libby in on my plan."

"Will do, and I mean, do I look like Tim McGraw?"

"In a way, you're taller, but I mean, do I look like Faith Hill?"

"In a way, but you're shorter."

They drove back to Irish Hills, and Goldie was feeling mighty proud of herself. If she couldn't put Irish Hills on the map due to her current career crisis, at least she could make it happen with Drake and his band.

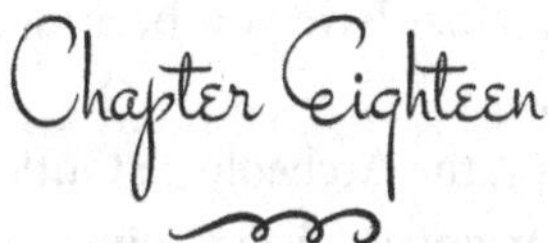

Chapter Eighteen

Goldie

Goldie watched in awe. Libby was a force! She had always been, but to see her now, with a project, a tight timetable, and her true mission, was impressive. She really could have been a producer.

"Okay, so, essentially, we have about twenty-four hours before country music's biggest stars show up downtown."

Libby had gathered the Sandbar Sisters, Aunt Emma, Keith, Joe, Dean, Jared, the old man who owned the grocery store, another gentleman who owned the local gas station, and about half a dozen others who she didn't know. They were meeting in the vacant retail space in the center of town.

"Hope, you're the key. They will be here for lunch and dinner. I know you laid off servers. Can you get them back for the weekend?"

"I can try. If not, Camila can find a few pinch hitters."

"Great."

"I need to get out of there and get moving, though. We're already behind."

"Yep," Libby said.

"And now the elephant in the room. What else are we going to have for them? I am one hundred percent a failure at getting additional retailers downtown."

"I mean, slacker. What have you been doing, eating bonbons, as they say?" J.J. said.

"My latest attempt, the Archeologie Outlet, was swooped away by Stirling Stone." Obviously, we're going to have a lovely restaurant for them, but what about this space?"

Goldie had done what she thought was needed. She had invited some big names to Irish Hills, but she didn't really understand the problems that might cause.

"I'm sorry, I thought I was, you know, helping."

"You did, and this is a good problem. We just want them to have more than a restaurant to tour."

"Let's make this a funky garage sale," Aunt Emma spoke up. For 90 years old, her voice was strong, and her ideas definitive.

"A funky garage sale?"

"You've got stuff in the attic at Nora House. For goodness' sake, there's a hundred years' worth of junk. My friends at the assisted living, we can fill this place with doodads and antiques."

"By tomorrow?"

"Yes, by tomorrow. If this meeting doesn't last much longer." Aunt Emma wasn't one to mince words. "Dean, I need your help to haul. Let's go."

J.J. stifled a giggle as Dean was commandeered by Aunt Emma.

A gentleman who owned a used car lot mentioned the classic car club he belonged to.

"I bet I can get an impromptu car show going. Those guys love to show off their babies."

"What do you need to make it happen?"

"Nothing, I'll do it over at the dealership."

"I love it," Libby said.

And one by one, the people in the room offered up their ideas and their contributions.

In less than an hour, they had a car show, Aunt Emma's funky garage sale, a quilt display in the courtyard gazebo, and a local jewelry maker was going to set up on the other end of Lake Manitou and Green Street. That would be at least three places to visit on the main drag. Libby had a clipboard, and she fielded everyone's questions and suggestions with aplomb. It was like a movie set, in a way.

Then Joe added his idea to the mix.

"I've got a storage unit full of holiday lights from a party tent business I used to run. I could string those up, maybe from the gazebo to the roof line on both sides. It would look like a very Hallmark movie downtown."

"That would be absolutely perfect. Do you need help?"

Libby's eyes went wide at the light idea. Lighting was a game changer. Goldie knew that from her lifetime in front of cameras.

"Just one other body to help me string 'em and hold a ladder."

"I'll do it!" Goldie could hold a ladder, if nothing else.

"Sold," Joe said.

Everyone scattered. They were determined to make Irish Hills a fun place, even if they didn't have a bunch of shops ready to dazzle the celebrity visitors about to descend.

As the meeting wrapped up, Goldie approached Libby.

"I hope this was okay, what I did?"

"Honey, it was perfect. And you just watch. By tomorrow, we'll have this downtown set up to welcome the second coming of Johnny Cash himself."

"You coming?" Joe was at the door, clearly ready to get started on the lights.

"I better get going. The boss is calling."

"He's a pretty handsome boss, by the way. He doesn't seem to be able to take his eyes off you."

Goldie smiled. She was used to being looked at. With Joe, it was different. He wasn't gawking. It was more like he was seeing her, not the movie star.

"I'll have to let this one down easy when the time comes." Goldie said the words and then felt immediately sad.

"Hmm, well, I hope it doesn't come for a while. I need those lights hung."

"I'm on it. Sorry I caused this, uh, well, fire drill."

"It's just what we need. That and a few social media posts from our visitors tomorrow, and I'm thinking Irish Hills will be on its way!"

Goldie's heart was full. She'd watched the town pull together at a moment's notice.

She spent the whirlwind next twenty-four hours doing whatever she could, from holding the ladder to assessing where more lights ought to be to watering flowers in the pots along the street.

At one point, she was going around pouring lemonade for volunteers who'd dropped everything to help Libby, and Irish Hills put its best face forward. She got a few double takes when people realized who she was, but they didn't lose it. She was here, just like they were, to help a friend, to save a little old town. It was one of the sweetest things she'd ever experienced.

It felt like she'd been transported back in time. It was the very opposite of what she was used to. If there was a cause, she wanted to support in L.A., she wrote a check. She'd do that here too if they asked, and had, with the hotel. Still, this was more satisfying.

Watching people lend a hand to each other to make the day special for anyone who visited melted her heart. She was surprised, at her age, that it was still possible.

Chapter Nineteen

Libby

By seven the next night, it was clear. Irish Hills was the place to be.

Well, it was the place to be in southern Michigan, at least, on this particular evening.

Goldie had thrown her a curve ball when she invited half of Nashville to town, but in the end, they'd pulled it off. It was the kind of boost Libby had been struggling to find.

Goldie was the catalyst, even though she couldn't be the draw. Her old friend had figured out a way to help them, even if it wasn't with a Film Festival or Goldie Hayes Fan weekend.

They'd pulled together everything at lightning speed. Libby hadn't slept since Goldie told her that Nashville was paying a visit to Irish Hills, but that was fine. She'd sleep after they pulled this off!

Traffic had started to pick up at noon, with a few recognizable country music celebrities, but they appeared with entourages and groupies. A slow trickle of tourists turned into a steady stream. By the evening, Irish Hills was literally hopping. People were strolling on the streets, checking out the car show, and taking selfies in the gazebo.

Aunt Emma's Attic, the pop-up funky garage sale her aunt had concocted, looked like a real store. J.J. had turned into a checkout clerk for a day. People oohed and aahed over the furniture, vintage clothes, and bobs and bits Emma and her band of senior citizens had on display. Libby had a vague concern Aunt Emma was going to sell something valuable for a few bucks, but she didn't have time to dwell on it.

Aunt Emma's Attic wasn't a permanent solution for the space, but it was enough to charm Courtney Caring. Courtney had a song climbing the charts and a huge Instagram following. She bought a hat, posted an adorable selfie with it, and tagged their location on the map. This was tourist town gold! Take that, Chef Ellston and Covert Pier.

The impromptu car show saw Luke Brush, country music's best bad boy, test driving a vintage Mustang down the main street while his girlfriend posted it to TikTok.

The best moment came that night, as Hope served a meal that got raves from the members of Burgundy Four and River Ann Flowers. They all tweeted pictures, and soon, Hope's Plate was trending on Twitter.

Libby was sitting at the bar at Hope's Plate with Keith. She was fairly certain it was the first time she'd sat down in over a day. He lifted his draft beer to her glass of red wine.

"Irish Hills is looking positively trendy."

"Ha, well, there's a lot of duct tape involved."

"Still, no one here seems to notice that. I heard that River Ann chick talking about filming a music video here."

Libby clasped her hands together to try to contain the excitement that was bubbling up inside her.

"You're cute when you're tickled pink." Keith leaned forward and gave her a peck on her forehead.

"Thanks. I am tickled. I just wonder about Goldie. She's my one worry right now."

"Why?"

"I'm not sure she knows that she should stay. I think she has one foot out the door back to L.A."

"If she's as smart as she seems, and if Joe turns on that charm, I'd say you don't have much to worry about."

Libby hoped that was true. While she wanted to enjoy the success, she did worry. That was the price you paid for caring about people: worry.

Hopefully, the Sandbar Sisters showed Goldie that no matter what was happening in her life, she had a safe place here.

Libby still had businesses to lure to fill the vacant buildings. She had plans for the buildings across the street that they hadn't touched yet. And there was the Lake View Dance Pavilion. She had so much to do!

But thankfully, all of a sudden, Irish Hills was looking a lot more appealing. It was practically cool. That was all Goldie. Her connections had made this happen.

"Can I buy your next rounds?" A man in jeans and a t-shirt who looked familiar stood between her and Keith. Familiar but different. Who in the...?

Whoa.

It was Stirling Stone. She'd only ever seen him clad in his business suit. She'd never seen him look so casual.

Libby noticed Keith's normally laid-back demeanor shift. Her enemy was his enemy, the clear message.

"Whoa, no thousand-dollar suit? Slumming today?"

"I am not. I'm here to concede."

"Concede?"

"I'm done trying to turn Irish Hills into a Stirling Stone Development property. You won at just about every turn. I know when I'm beaten."

Libby had to shake her head to be sure she heard right. It had to be another ploy of his.

"I'm assuming this is your latest tactic. Maybe one of your subsidiaries is going to start pushing to buy up the properties?"

"No, if I buy something, I buy something. I'm not hiding that. But if you want to call Mayor Eastland, you'll see Grant Mills has submitted the paperwork to withdraw the request for a second eminent domain hearing."

"You got Archeologie Outlet to select Covert Pier. You won that one, not me."

"That was a tiny thing. Look around. You won. I mean, the lead singer of Burgundy Four is about to propose to River Ann Daisy or whatever her name is, at that table in the corner."

"River Ann Flowers," Libby corrected.

Keith, Libby, and Stirling looked over to the corner table and saw that Stirling Stone was correct. Drake was on one knee. River Ann Flowers' army of girlfriends were taking videos with their phones. It was a whole thing. It was all happening in Irish Hills, the place to be!

"Yes! Yes!"

The restaurant erupted in applause as River Ann Flowers gushed over her new ring.

Libby turned back to Stirling Stone. She narrowed her eyes. What was his game?

"No stopping it now. You have turned Irish Hills into its own little tourist town, not my idea of a resort. But like I said, I know when I'm beaten."

"Forgive me if I don't believe you."

Stirling Stone shrugged, and then he smiled. The man's teeth were so white they almost glowed.

"This was fun, sparring with you. It's been eye opening to be surprised, and Irish Hills has surprised me at every turn."

"And you're not going to try to takeover because we're surprising?"

"I see what you've fostered here, they want to do things your way. They want to save the town too, you just helped them realize it. That's a lot to fight against."

Libby had the feeling she was sticking her hand outside of a shark cage. The smile, the concession, the affable demeanor; these were all designed to make her let her guard down. Stirling Stone was ready, willing, and able to bite off her hand.

"What about Covert Pier? Maybe that's your game, siphon every idea we have over to them?" Libby's mind was racing. What was he trying to do by telling her she won?

"I have an investment with Chef Ellston, but that's for my Vegas hotel. Covert Pier is booming on its own. No agenda. I promise."

Libby was in fight mode. She was not ready to relax or celebrate that they had vanquished Stirling Stone.

"So, no hearing request? I will call Mayor Eastland."

"Actually, I think he's over there, having a drink with the drummer from Burgundy Four."

Libby looked over, and sure enough, the mayor was, in fact, partying with the band.

Stirling Stone, billionaire, dropped cash on the bar for their drinks. He nodded to Keith and Libby and then left as quickly as he'd appeared. Libby was unsettled. Her mind, always churning with ideas to fend off Stone, didn't switch gears so easily.

Surely, he had some ulterior motive. This had to be a trick. Still, maybe they had done it. Maybe they had caused just enough trouble to be too much trouble for the billionaire.

"What do you know about that?" Libby asked Keith.

"I'm not surprised in the least."

"Not surprised that one of the most powerful men in the country just called uncle?"

"Only a fool gets between Libby Quinn and whatever it is she's got her heart set on."

"Yeah, well, then, don't be a fool." Libby leaned in and kissed Keith on the cheek.

"Yes, ma'am."

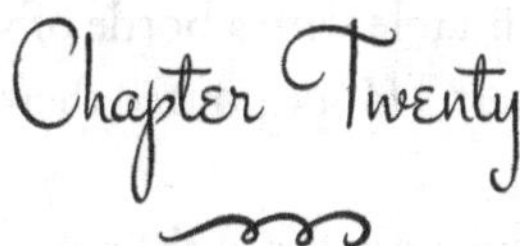

Chapter Twenty

Goldie

Goldie was out in the world again. At least a little. She'd been all over town helping during the setup. And Joe convinced her to come to dinner.

Goldie wasn't trying to disguise herself, but she also wasn't giving full movie star vibes. She banked on the fact that the biggest names in country music were crawling all over Irish Hills. She was an afterthought.

Hope had set her up at a corner table in the back. No one was paying attention to her. She wasn't exactly sure how to feel about that. Regardless, it was nice to see the fruits of their work over the last day.

"Wow, your old boyfriend there, proposing to that teenager. Kind of gross if you ask me."

Goldie laughed. Drake was too old for River Ann, but she was hardly a teen.

"She's not a teenager, but she is half his age, but only a third of his age if you go by how old he says he is."

"What kind of math is that now?"

"Hollywood male math, trust me, it's indecipherable."

"I'd say you did well here, Miss Hayes."

"Thank you."

Hope came to their table with a bottle of wine.

"Cherry Creek's best." Hope poured them both a glass.

"Cherry Creek?"

"Yep, we have several wineries in the area, a regular Napa Valley in Lenawee County."

"There's a lot more here to love than I realized," Goldie said as she took a sip of the wine. It was better than she'd expected. Over her wine glass she caught a glance between Hope and Joe. Oh, oops. She was in "like," maybe in "lust," but not in love with Joe Cassidy. She didn't mean to imply that! Plus, she had a life to get back to in L.A. after the nonsense with Victor fanboys died down.

For tonight, she'd enjoy success with her friends. Libby's work for Irish Hills was nothing short of a miracle. Hope would already be a sensation if this place was in L.A. But now that it was getting some love from the country music crowd, hopefully the locals would also discover it.

The idea of leaving her old friends, not to mention the pure joy that was being in J.J.'s orbit, formed a dark cloud in Goldie's mind. Still, her life was there, not here.

But for now, she'd laugh with her friends, flirt with Joe, and enjoy wine from Michigan, of all places!

Her phone, however, had other plans. It started vibrating. Over and over and over again.

She was about to pull it out of her purse to see why.

At that moment, J.J. appeared with a look of concern.

"Hey, Sister, there's a group there, waiting for a table. They do not look like the country music crowd." J.J. had blocked their view but now slowly slid to the side for Goldie to get a better look. "They're wearing superhero t-shirts."

"Shoot, I'm probably in the background of some of these shots getting posted. I really did let my guard down."

"Hope says you can sneak out that way through the kitchen."

"Come on, I'll get you out of here," Joe said.

So much for eating a meal in public. The fanboys were relentless. Joe stood first. He was twice her size. He easily blocked the view for any gawking diners as they slid behind the bar and back to Hope's bustling kitchen.

"This way," Hope said. And she opened a screen door at the back of the kitchen and held it open for them. Joe went out first and looked left and right like they were in a spy movie.

"Thanks, Hope."

"Yep, I'll try to slow them up, get 'em seated, and serve 'em slow."

Joe reached his hand out and led Goldie as they walked around the restaurant to the sidewalk. Goldie liked holding hands with Joe. Even though she did not like the fact that they had to flee the restaurant.

The truck was in sight when another group of fans jumped between them and her escape.

"Found her!"

"Will you sign this? Can we get a selfie? Are you going to do a Steely Ann standalone movie?"

"Uh, what?" Goldie tried to decipher the rapid-fire questions.

Joe pulled her behind him as if they were actually throwing stuff at her like they had at the convention. She'd expected vegetables flying, not autograph requests.

"I'll sign. It's okay."

Joe reluctantly stood down as she signed a t-shirt and autograph book and then posed for a picture.

"Thank you! Oh my, God!" The fans were thrilled, apparently. And after they got what they'd come for, they moved out of the way for Joe and Goldie to get to the truck.

They looked like the same VSU fan contingent, but they sure

didn't act like the typical VSU fan, blaming Goldie for ruining, well, everything.

"That was weird."

"Well, they clearly love your work."

"Yeah, but they didn't hurl insults or accuse me of destroying their entire superhero world."

"A more mature mutation of Victor fanboy?"

"Maybe."

It was then that she remembered her phone had been blowing up earlier.

As Joe weaved through the relatively congested traffic situation in downtown Irish Hills, she pulled out her phone.

There were missed calls from Hedda. And several texts from Tally.

She decided to call Tally first. Let the agent wait.

Tally answered immediately. "Oh good, I need to know how you want me to respond, schedule-wise and all that?"

"To what?"

"Well, in the last twenty-four hours, you've got twelve endorsement requests, six talk show appearance requests, a script, and two requests from the head of the VSU and, uh, yeah, the new CEO of Disney."

"What, how?"

"I don't know. It's all I can do to keep up."

"Okay, you've forwarded everything important to my private email?"

"Yes, I didn't bother you with the stuff I know you're not into."

"Okay, just keep doing that. And I'll check back in after I sort it out."

She hung up with Tally.

"Good news?" Joe asked.

"I don't know. I'd been untouchable for the last few weeks,

and now all of a sudden, I'm the belle of the ball. And I'm not even there."

She dialed Hedda, who was technically not her agent.

"Well, there she is, the woman of the hour."

"Hedda, what is going on? I'm being flooded with offers, and a pack of fanboys just asked for autographs instead of asking for my head on a platter."

"I told you how I was going to ask around about how your scenes looked in Trevor's mess of a movie?"

"Yes."

"Well, a couple of things on that front. Trevor Sunday has been fired for myriad reasons. To begin with, after seeing the dailies, the studio became incredibly concerned about having him at the helm of a huge tent pole movie in the VSU franchise."

"Can't say I'm sad about that."

"But wait, there's more."

"Yeah?"

"The best thing about the mess of a movie was you."

"What?"

"Yeah, the only scenes that work are the scenes you're in. And your big line, it's perfection. The rest of it is crap, total crap. But you save what's left. So much so that the powers that be in the VSU want to talk about Steely Ann having her own movie."

"And this is widely known now?"

"Yes, it broke in the *Hollywood Reporter*. I've been trying to get you on the phone for hours."

"Karma rarely works this fast."

"I need you back in town now."

"Laying low seems to be working well for me. Why don't I extend into the fall?"

"Striking while the iron is hot is also a thing, and the iron is white hot for you right now."

"Listen, we haven't even signed an agreement."

"Another reason for you to take a meeting with me. I'll make sure to work around your schedule."

Goldie's schedule was wide open. But she wasn't going to let Hedda know that.

"I'll have Tally reach out with availability."

"So, you're coming back to town?"

"Early next week work?"

"Perfect, see you then."

They ended the call.

"Headed back to Hollywood, eh?"

"Is it that obvious?"

"I got the gist. What about the hotel?"

"I haven't thought that far out. We don't have bookings yet. There's a lot to do on your end for maintenance. I can't imagine it will be ready until next season, realistically?"

"True."

She didn't want to bring up the other elephant in the room, their budding relationship.

Except it wasn't a relationship. They'd kissed. They'd flirted. She was too old and too jaded to think it was some sort of great love.

He didn't bring it up, either.

Goldie needed to get back to her life, or else she'd have no life to get back to. Hedda was right. The iron was hot. And she had been around long enough to know, when it happened, you jumped.

Chapter Twenty-One

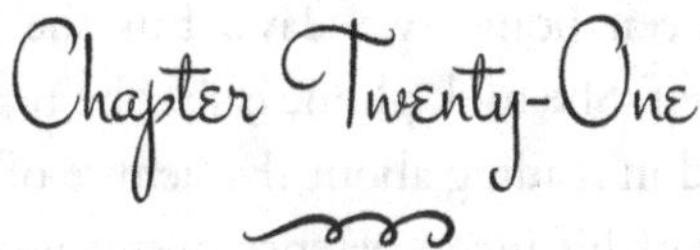

Goldie

She'd said hasty goodbyes... all over the phone. It was easier that way. She'd dropped into the lives of her old friends out of nowhere, and now, she'd dropped back out.

Goldie tried not to feel like she'd abandoned them. In truth, she didn't know what her obligation to her friends really was. Did she owe them more? All she could manage were swift, non-dramatic conversations. She was cutting ties that were merely temporary to begin with.

She had made Irish Hills better, she hoped, while she was there.

And there was Joe, in the hotel she owned, still working on the projects they'd agreed on. She didn't say goodbye to him. They'd just left it all open.

Or maybe it was closed. He went back to his work, and she went back to hers. He didn't try to stop her. She was grateful for that. Clingy was not attractive.

She wondered what Joe would think of her Trousdale house.

It was pristine, not a dust bunny to be found. And certainly not a raccoon. But Myrna, her sweet, spoiled doggie was there. That's all she needed. Her puppy, her mansion, and the power to bend studio heads to her will. So little to ask for.

Goldie had been home two days. But she felt off, like she wasn't quite herself. She took phone calls. She read industry news. She even indulged in reading about the demise of Trevor Sunday's career. The story of his incompetence on set wasn't news to her, but it was interesting to see that she wasn't the only one who noticed.

She also had a friend she didn't expect. The makeup artist who had witnessed Trevor ask Goldie to film the degrading scene, where Greased Lightning was supposed to fall on top of her, had shared that story. Victor Superhero Universe fans were outraged that Trevor Scott would try to make Steely Ann look like a clown, and her fellow actresses were praising her for refusing to do it.

But the victory over Victor would have been sweeter, if shared with her friends. She could almost hear J.J. demanding a high five. She had started to feel more at home in the back bedroom of the Two Lakes Grove than she did in the primary suite of her mansion, which was large enough to land a helicopter in.

Maybe because it was quiet. Too quiet. And empty. Her house, in the late summer in L.A., managed to be cold. And Myrna loved her, but the dog had boundaries, and got grumpy with too much fussing.

Tally had arranged for a new driver and security, as Goldie had instructed. Tally had also turned in her resignation.

"I loved working for you, but I didn't know how long you'd be gone. So, I floated my name out there."

"It's okay, I understand. I didn't know either."

"But I don't start the tour until next month. I'll do everything I can to make sure you're all set."

"I appreciate it, and it will be a blast."

Tally was young. Going on tour with a rock band would be

fun. She'd been hired as an assistant to the tour manager. It sounded like pure hell to Goldie, but then Goldie was not young, and now, as she closed in on fifty, she realized she was positively ancient.

Except, when she was back home, in Irish Hills, she didn't feel so ancient.

Home? Her mind had switched home from her mansion in California to her beat-up hotel in Michigan. That wasn't home. What in the world?

As she paced, her standard method of dealing with things, she realized what control of her career could really mean. She realized what she wanted before she went to Irish Hills wasn't the same as what she wanted now.

She had new demands. And if Hedda was right, she could get exactly what she wanted.

* * *

Goldie had prepped all morning for the lunch with her new prospective agent.

Goldie wore a designer dress, a short bodycon number in mango. She paired it with nude, sky high Louboutins. She'd look fierce in photos, and she knew there would be photos. She counted on it. She looked down at the fancy shoes and laughed. A memory of Joe raising his eyebrow at her wardrobe popped in her head.

Goldie had Tally accompany her to the restaurant for the meeting. But only for appearances. Tally was there to make Goldie look like she had an entourage. Tally was her people. This was a role she was playing, of the movie star.

Tally had already tipped off the paparazzi, at Goldie's request, that she was going to be lunching with a power player. She even encouraged Tally to collect the bounty that was offered for Goldie Hayes sightings. If people were going to snitch to the press where she was, it might as well be on her own terms.

Her new driver pulled up to the entrance of The Ivy. He assisted Goldie, and then Tally scurried around the car from the other door to make it look like they were in a huge hurry. She also parted the way for Goldie, as if she couldn't get through without a team of people. A scrum of paparazzi surged forward as she tried to enter the restaurant.

"What do you think of Trevor getting the ax?"

"Did you have a good vacation?"

"What's your reaction to Drake's engagement to River Ann?"

"Are you going to sue the VSU for defamation?"

She smiled pleasantly but kept walking. The real story they would get is the view of her meeting with Hedda. Hedda was up and coming. And this meeting would cement the idea that Hedda was the agent to have, not Scott Ozock. That was the point of the pictures. She wanted the power to be firmly in her hands, and Hedda's.

Goldie knew if she wasn't with Ozock, Hedda was the best and only other way to go. Anything else would look like a failure. A boutique agency was a step-down. She knew her value. And now, with the tide turned on Trevor, she could capitalize on it.

Hedda was beautifully dressed. Her enviable curves filled out a white pencil skirt. She'd cinched it with a wide patent leather belt and topped it with a gorgeous black silk blouse. Hedda also looked intimidating, which was what Goldie wanted in an agent.

Hedda greeted Goldie as though they were best friends. The two women sat at a table by the window. This was not an accident.

Hedda got right to the point. Goldie liked that, too.

"Okay, so, you're obviously aware we have the power. You're actually the first person I've ever seen put the Victor Superhero Universe machine over a barrel like this."

"One of the questions out there was about me suing. Do you know what that's about?"

"Well, they let Trevor defame you. The company didn't stop him from lying to the press about why they were actually having problems with the movie. They should have been defending you when he ran his mouth off and cost you work and reputation."

"Ah, you know, in all this time, I didn't even think about that."

"Well, they also don't know that. I may have floated the story that you were looking to hire Arie Shore."

Arie Shore was a shark of a different stripe. He was an attorney you did not want to deal with, but the best kind if he was on your side.

"Oooh, now that's good. That's very good."

"What do you want to make this happen? I want to announce that you're coming over to my agency ASAP. I want to bring you on officially."

"I want to know you're in line with what I see next for myself."

"Oh, you're going to be able to lead the Victor Superhero Universe. You'll be bigger than General Patriot. The back-end deals I've got in mind, and a cut of the merchandising, it's life-changing money."

General Patriot was the leader of the VSU pantheon. Steely Ann, more powerful than General Patriot? That was hilarious. That could be interesting. Goldie had a mission with this meeting, and usurping superheroes wasn't it.

"I have all the money I need."

"Yeah, but you know this town. Money isn't money. It's power."

"True, and that's all great." Goldie knew in Hollywood; lucrative deals were important. They made people think you were in charge. Demanding compensation was commanding respect.

"I can get you the first look at whatever script you're interested in. We can go lifestyle brand, book deal, whatever speaks to you."

She'd been thinking a lot about what she wanted. What did she really need from Hollywood at this stage of her life?

Goldie had been fighting to stay on top of a pile.

She'd climbed up here and then had to keep fighting to stay. And a lot of the time, certainly since Mitchell Ozock died, she'd been losing the fight. She'd also been fighting alone. Her team was all people she paid. She didn't have a true support network, a real team.

She loved her career. She loved what she'd accomplished. But being in Irish Hills, with her friends, with people who actually cared about her, who, instead of capitalizing on her fame, protected her, opened her eyes.

Libby had reached out to Goldie because she wanted something from her. In the end, Goldie had gotten something from Libby, Hope, and J.J., something she needed and didn't even know it.

Goldie wanted a different path for the next part of her life. The last two days back in L.A., she felt like a stranger in a strange land. Like a visitor in her old life.

Goldie had thought about it. And she decided what she wanted next. And once she did, it was easy. Things would fall into place the way they were supposed to.

"I'm going to make some changes in my life. I would love it if you were the right person for this new path I'm going to be on. I'm going to tell you and also let you know that it's not negotiable. If this works for you, great. If it doesn't, then it's not supposed to."

"Very Zen of you,"

"Not sure if it's Zen or just middle age, but I'm going to pull a Jeff Daniels here."

"What? He's not in the Victor Superhero Universe. Do you want to get him to star in your next project?"

"Ah, no, I mean sure. But that's not it. A few years before I moved out of Michigan to Hollywood, Jeff Daniels did the exact opposite. He was nominated for Oscars, well respected, and all that, but decided to run his career from Michigan, not California."

"Uh, okay, but I'm not really following."

"I am moving to Michigan permanently. I'm going to limit my shooting schedule to the winter months, maybe a touch into March. But April to, oh, November or so, I'll be running my little inn in Michigan. Oh, and I'm not going to ever take a role again where the requirement is losing weight. I'm eating what I want. Actually, where's our server?"

"What about the VSU, about your own franchise?"

"I'm okay with that, but on my terms. If they can't work with my terms, that's fine, too. I'll do smaller pictures. Actually, that's the next part of my vision."

"I'm listening."

"I will be buying up rights, when I can, to books I like, with the express purpose of turning them into movies."

"Ah, so we're morphing into Winnie Reese with books and Jeff Daniels with the Michigan thing?"

"No, I have no illusion that I can be either. I just want to be me in a place that values that instead of trying to sell it. I want to be in a town that feels like home and not one that feels like a snake pit."

"Ah, well, you've done pretty well in the snake pit."

"I just know where I'm going for the next bit and who I want to have with me."

"I see."

"Do you want to come along, or do I sort of wing it? I've done that before."

Hedda sat forward in her chair. She locked eyes with Goldie.

"I'm in. I would be nuts to say no to the most powerful woman in Hollywood."

"Today, I'm the most powerful woman today; tomorrow, it will be someone else."

"Then today's the day for you to make this deal."

"I look forward to working with you."

"I think this is the beginning of the best part of your career. I know it is."

"I think it's the beginning of the best part of my life."

* * *

The summer had turned a corner. Leaves were green; still, the middle of the day was hot, and the boats were on the lake.

But leaves were falling, a few at a time, enough to remind you this was all fleeting. A new season was coming. The light in the evening was burnished gold as the sunset, changed from the blazing orange of July.

Goldie had been back for a week. She'd reunited with Joe. She'd kissed him a time or two even, but that was also in a season to come. The season of whatever they'd be together was ahead of them. She was looking forward to it but not rushing it. And he was letting her set their pace. He was getting used to Myrna. Myrna was tolerating him.

Myrna did seem to like barking at ducks that swam by on the lake. All in all, Myrna Loy was settling in just as Goldie was.

Goldie had spent just about every moment with Joe since she'd gotten back. He was happy to see her, and he told her so. It was sweet, easy, and more mutual than any other romance she'd ever been in. She was just starting to realize the benefits of dating a man who wasn't a celebrity or who had any desire to be one.

Over the last several days, Joe had helped her turn the first-floor sitting room, the dining room, and her own bedroom at Two Lakes Grove into something lovely. It was crisp white, and the floors, now free of carpet, looked beautiful. They were slowly uncovering the history of the place, bringing it to life with each little project.

Two Lakes Grove was far from being done. Goldie looked forward to each paint color decision, each piece of art for the walls, and each step she still had to take to make Two Lakes spectacular.

But there was no deadline. For the first time in her life, she was savoring each slow second.

"You need anything else? Before your girls get here?"

"No, I think I'm good to go. Have you checked on the new fridge? It's still doing the job?"

"It is. It looks totally out of place since we haven't redone the kitchen yet, but it's chilling your cheese and chardonnay."

"That's all I need for today."

"All you need?"

"Maybe not all I need."

Joe took her hand and actually kissed it. Chivalry wasn't dead. It just wasn't in L.A. It was alive and well and thriving on a lazy lake in Michigan.

Goldie's demands of the VSU had been met. Each one. Even a few that she threw in just to test them were green lit. She would be flying in and out in the winter, at their expense, for her next project. The VSU honchos had given her everything Hedda asked for.

Joe didn't blink when she explained who she was, how she had planned to try to have the best of both of her worlds. He didn't ask her to change her life for his. She offered him the same consideration. If they were meant to be, and she did hope they were, it would work out.

He also knew how to make himself scarce when the Sandbar Sisters were rolling in for a girl's night.

Goldie had invited the Sandbar Sisters, along with Aunt Emma, to come over for dinner and drinks. They had a lot to catch up on.

J.J. arrived first. Her old friend had been researching how to get Goldie's hair the color it needed to be to finish the VSU shoot in the winter. J.J. had all the tools and skills Goldie needed to be camera ready, to her delight. Goldie thought, at the very least, she'd be driving to Ann Arbor for some of her hair and makeup requirements. Goldie needed a lot of maintenance, whether she was here or in L.A., but J.J. was rising to the challenge. Goldie was even hoping to convince J.J. to come on location this winter. One of her many demands was that the VSU studio hire the hair and makeup artists she selected. Why not J.J.?

"Look, I'm here to tell you that I can be your full-service hair stylist, but if I'm ever off, do not let Shelly touch you. I promise she'll convince you to do an inverted bob, and you'll regret it for the rest of your life."

"Check."

Libby and Hope arrived next. A dish in Hope's hands made Goldie realize she'd not complied with Goldie's edict not to bring anything.

"It's a leftover. I literally did nothing."

Goldie knew that was a lie. "I promise, I had this food delivered. We're in no danger of poisoning."

She guided them into the grand lobby and sitting room.

"Wow, just paint, and getting that carpet up has turned this lobby into a showplace!"

"I even helped pull off the carpet. It was the first real test of my true compatibility with Joe."

"And?"

"He only wanted to kill me once, so I think that's a great sign."

"Oh, I hear Aunt Emma's car."

Goldie went back to the door and saw a distinguished-looking man get out of the driver's seat, open the door for Aunt Emma, and then help her out.

Goldie reached out a hand to assist the older woman in navigating the steps into the hotel.

"This place is looking grander by the day. Lovely!"

Aunt Emma joined the Sandbar Sisters in the lobby to appreciate the progress.

"I just realized why that man who was driving you looked familiar, Aunt Emma. That was the man who almost bought this place out from under me."

"What?" Aunt Emma's eyes opened wide, and she blinked.

If Goldie knew one thing, it was when someone was acting. Aunt Emma was acting innocent.

"He's the one who was going to make all those garish changes to this place. The one who I beat out to buy it."

"Aunt Emma, what did you cook up?" Libby chimed in.

"Nothing, nothing."

"What was his name? Oh yeah, Tate Patrick, a hotel developer from Ann Arbor," Goldie said as the details came back to her.

"Oh, brother." Libby put her head in her hand.

"You sly boots!" J.J. exclaimed.

Hope looked as baffled as Goldie felt.

"Look, he would have bought it if he could..." Aunt Emma started.

"—Aunt Emma, you hoodwinked Goldie!" Libby was angry.

Goldie was not quite sure what had happened. "Hoodwinked? I just did a major deal in Hollywood. I doubt Aunt Emma was able to hoodwink me." She stepped over to the older woman and put an arm around her.

"Do you want to fess up, or am I going to bust you?" Libby pressed.

Aunt Emma frowned. She narrowed her eyes and then tilted her head. "Fine, I'll share. My dear niece, you're so by the book sometimes it's just limiting." Aunt Emma turned to Goldie. "His name is Patrick Tate, not Tate Patrick. We came up with his alias on the fly. It's not great, I see."

"And?"

"And, I had him pretend to want to buy this place and do the tackiest things we could think of, so you'd get the stick out of your—"

"—Aunt Emma!"

"Sorry, niece. Um, so you'd not be a stick in the mud and buy this hotel. Like you should have from day one."

"I'm so sorry, Goldie," Libby said. "I had no idea she had concocted this scheme. I am horrified that you were lured into buying this place under false pretenses."

Aunt Emma looked at Goldie with her innocent eyes. The rest of her Sandbar Sisters seemed to be holding their breath. Was the temperamental movie star going to storm out? Was she merely a fair-weather fan of Irish Hills?

"Oh, the drama! Aunt Emma, you are quite the actress."

"I'd understand if you want to pull out. I can't swing re-buying it from you right now, but I'll put a plan in place. I'm so sorry," Libby was babbling. That was not normal Libby.

"Not a chance. You're all stuck with me, well, at least in the summer months."

"Oh, thank goodness." Aunt Emma let out a sigh. "La La Land hasn't fried your brain. You have good sense!"

"I don't know how wise it is to chuck my life and start a new one at my age, but I'm doing it."

They circled her in hugs. Goldie didn't even try to deflect the affection from her friends. She didn't need to have armor here.

"I need a glass of Chardonnay for the road. I can't stay," Aunt Emma said.

"What?"

"You're not the only ones with silver foxes at your beck and call."

"Aunt Emma," Libby gasped.

"He's a younger man but over seventy. It's my experience men are too immature before seventy to be much use. Oh, except for lifting furniture. Other than that, pfft."

Goldie gave Aunt Emma a glass of Chardonnay. She drank it down in one gulp.

Before she took her leave, Aunt Emma looked Goldie square in the eyes. She pulled her in close and spoke quietly. "You're doing the right thing, making a life here. It's the best decision you ever made. Well, maybe the second best, according to Viv."

"You keep in touch with her?"

"Now and again." Aunt Emma hugged her and said her goodbyes.

They settled on chairs out back and watched boaters lazily motor by as the sun set.

The food was delicious. Goldie didn't count one single carb or calorie as she ate it.

"So, what was that about the second-best decision?" J.J. asked.

It was a secret between her and Viv, one that no one but them knew. But it was time to tell her sisters, the ones who would also have been there for her, she knew now, if only she had asked.

"I have a twenty-two-year-old daughter."

"What? Congratulations! I mean, oh my goodness, that's wonderful!" Hope enthused.

"Look, I know your IMBD bio down to the last comma. You'd have been in *People Magazine*. Not one whiff of this has ever been reported," J.J. said.

"Yeah, true. Well, a long time ago, I fell in love with a famous man, and I got pregnant. He said it would ruin his career. He was married."

"What a jerk," J.J. said.

"I was in a tough spot. It could have ruined my career, too. I had a lot of resources, thanks to my movie paychecks, just not a lot of support. The smartest thing I did, maybe ever, was call an old friend."

"Oh my gosh." Libby had started to piece it together. Goldie hadn't called any one of them, and they were the oldest of friends. "Viv, you called Viv!"

"I did. After I went out to Hollywood, we kept in touch. She was starting her design career, doing some styling. She was having fertility issues, and I was not, turns out."

"Wow, Viv, I miss her. We need to concoct a reason to get her out here like we did these two," J.J. said.

"She's happily divorced, living in New York State, with our daughter."

"Our daughter?" Hope said.

"Viv left the terms of the adoption up to me, so it's open. I'm Aunt Goldie, but Siena knows I'm her biological mother. Viv has been generous with their lives. But it was Viv who did the raising. Viv is her mom. I'm Aunt Goldie."

She was a little sad when she said it. She didn't mean to be. It had worked out. Siena had a beautiful life. While Goldie had taken center stage in the movies, she was in the wings of Siena's life. And that's the way it should be for kids. They should be the star, not the satellite.

Libby stood up and walked over to Goldie. She crouched down and wrapped her friend in a hug. Soon, J.J. and Hope were smashing Goldie with a love bomb.

"Wow, what was that for?"

"First, that you let us hug you now! It's nice to see your guard down. And second, I'm glad we're all back in each other's lives," said Libby.

"Oh, and third, we didn't get to back then, when you and Viv did this amazing thing," J.J. added.

"Okay, I'm opening another bottle of wine. I want to hear *all* about Siena. She's got to be brilliant," Hope announced.

They finished off another bottle, all the food Goldie had ordered, and even dessert.

They planned what was next for the hotel and how to get the word out about it. Next summer was going to be so different from this summer. If they played it right, Irish Hills and Two Lakes Grove would be packed!

The Sandbar Sisters talked about nearly everything under the sun. They kicked around the idea of a film festival. Hope raved about how well Keith's son was doing at the restaurant. J.J. pushed back against the suggestion that she open a salon at the other end of Green Street and they all brainstormed what type of retail would work long-term in the center space.

They also giggled, like they did when they were girls, over Joe, Keith, and Greg. All of them were in the throes of a new romance, which was just as fun as back when they were girls. There wasn't a better place on earth, Goldie decided. Nor better people.

She had a contract to sign for a movie to be shot in Toronto this winter. She had three lovely books to read to consider for rights acquisition. And she had a hotel to fix up. All of it glorious. All of it exactly what she wanted to be doing.

She took another bite of the bread that Hope had brought. It was warm and fluffy, and completely divine. She realized, for the first time in a long time, maybe ever, Goldie was full.

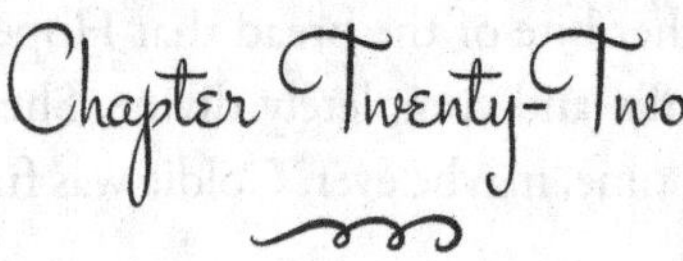

Chapter Twenty-Two

Viv, Two Months Later

Viv knew the phone call wasn't a good one.

It had come so soon after the tests. That meant it was urgent.

Urgent wasn't good.

She'd acted as though she had no inkling of what was to come on the drive to the hospital. She knew Siena was nervous enough for both of them.

Why make the possible last normal moments they shared weird by bringing on the gloom that could very likely settle over their lives? She knew the drive home would be different. At least now, in this space, she could pretend she didn't know.

The leaves were turning. She usually loved autumn. Would she hate autumn now? Is that how it worked? If they put a song on the radio right now, would they then always be sad when they heard that song?

They kept the radio off.

She appreciated her daughter more than ever at this moment. Her daughter was so smart, thoughtful, and calm. Well, outwardly calm. Siena chatted about colors for the new scarves and a pallet for spring dresses. Viv knew this was Siena's way of coping with the weight of whatever came next. Siena was a grown-up. How had that happened?

Her daughter was beautiful inside and out. She had Goldie's smile. When Siena flashed a smile, it dazzled. That was pure Goldie Hayes. But Siena was longer, her coloring darker than Goldie's. She was her own gorgeous creature.

Libby passed the time in the car thinking about changing leaves and memorizing her daughter's face. They arrived at the hospital, and her nerves were manageable. She wasn't exactly calm, but she was okay.

They walked to the office, meandered really. No need to rush this news.

Viv and Siena sat in chairs across from Dr. Hinkley. She'd seen Dr. Hinkley since they'd moved here. That had to be twenty years now. Twenty years ago, when Siena was a toddler. Maybe Viv should have called Bret, had him come with her.

Bret was her ex-husband, but her closest friend—well, really, still family. Was it unfair to lean on her girl for this?

She didn't know what was right. Bret maybe would have forgotten to ask the right questions. Siena would ask the right questions. They'd come out of here with an exact picture of what to do next.

Dr. Hinkley looked grim. Or maybe Viv was projecting her own state of mind onto her doctor. Maybe she was just serious. Viv didn't trust her own perceptions. That was weird. Perceiving the world, and interpreting it, was art. She was an artist.

But right now, she was a woman with a lump in front of a doctor with the news.

"Okay, we're here. We're ready," Viv said.

"Well, I suppose you've already guessed. The biopsy wasn't what we'd hoped."

Siena reached out a hand to her, and Viv took it. She squeezed.

She was feeling okay, strong for the moment, strong enough to hear what she knew was coming next.

"It is cancer."

It sank in for a second, that word. Every time a doctor called, she feared that cancer was the reason: oh hey, that headache is cancer, that cough, cancer, that funny lump in your breast, cancer.

And it never was until it is.

But cancer could be anything these days. It could be life or death. It wasn't like with her mom. She squeezed out that memory. That wouldn't serve her well right now. Viv was going to have to do a lot of visualizing. Positive visualizing would help. Conjuring memories of her mother's worst days would hurt.

She took a deep breath and asked the question.

"How bad?"

"Not the best, but not the worst. The tumor is around three centimeters, and we've got one lymph node involved."

There, that ripped off the band-aid, her cancer had already spread.

"What does that mean?"

"It means we've got a fight, but it's one I know we can win."

Viv took it in. She wondered what a fight meant to Dr. Hinkley. Viv already ate healthily, she exercised, she didn't drink, well, didn't drink much. She'd done all of the things.

Except...

Her mother. Her mother died of this. Her mother died of this. She squeezed away the memory. That was not the mantra she should chant.

The doctor began to say words that had no meaning. She'd need to look them up. Viv would understand all she needed to. She would be an active participant in this fight. No doubt about it. But right now, she felt disconnected from it. Were they talking about her?

She felt fine. That would change, but right now, she felt fine. Odd.

Viv looked out the window as her daughter, and the doctor continued to talk.

There would be time to learn all of this. She would know more about it than she wanted to, she supposed.

The window overlooked the neighborhood next to the hospital. This had to be peak fall color. Orange, burgundy, yellow, brown, they were all there, right below them. She would love to paint that. Or find a fabric with those colors.

She remembered autumn in Michigan. Out of the blue, the smell of apples came to her mind. Libby and Hope used to drive all five of them to get apples and cider. Libby had a car. Viv didn't then. Ha, funny the things that pop into your mind when you're trying to disassociate from the actual moment you're trapped in.

Sandbar Sister memories were never too far away these days. She wondered why that was. Maybe because they were pure fun, pure youth, just pure.

Viv forced herself back to the present, to the conversation that was going on about her.

Her daughter was listening, taking the pamphlets offered. Viv knew she needed to engage in this. She knew she'd be required to understand it all in detail. She would do that. She would. But right now, just looking out the window was what she could manage. She wanted to see the colors. Maybe she'd get out her paints this afternoon, after this appointment.

Maybe not, maybe she'd go for a walk.

It was hard to say what she would do, one minute to the next.

Her daughter asked about timing and who to schedule with. The details were all there to be arranged, the front desk, a surgeon. There were pamphlets and numbers for support. It was a club, she saw, a club of people who heard this same news.

Thank goodness for Siena. Siena was listening and handling it.

Viv would, too, soon.

Very soon, she'd be in the fight.

But for now, she looked out the window at the leaves on the trees.

The Story Continues in Sandbar Storm

Also by Rebecca Regnier

Summer Cottage Novels

- Sandbar Sisters
- Sandbar Season
- Sandbar Summer
- Sandbar Storm
- Sandbar Sunset

Widow's Bay Paranormal Women's Fiction Mysteries

North of Forty-Nine Paranormal Women's Fiction Adventure

Kendra Dillon Suspense Thrillers (As Rebecca Rane)